MEET THE MASTERS OF SPINJITZU

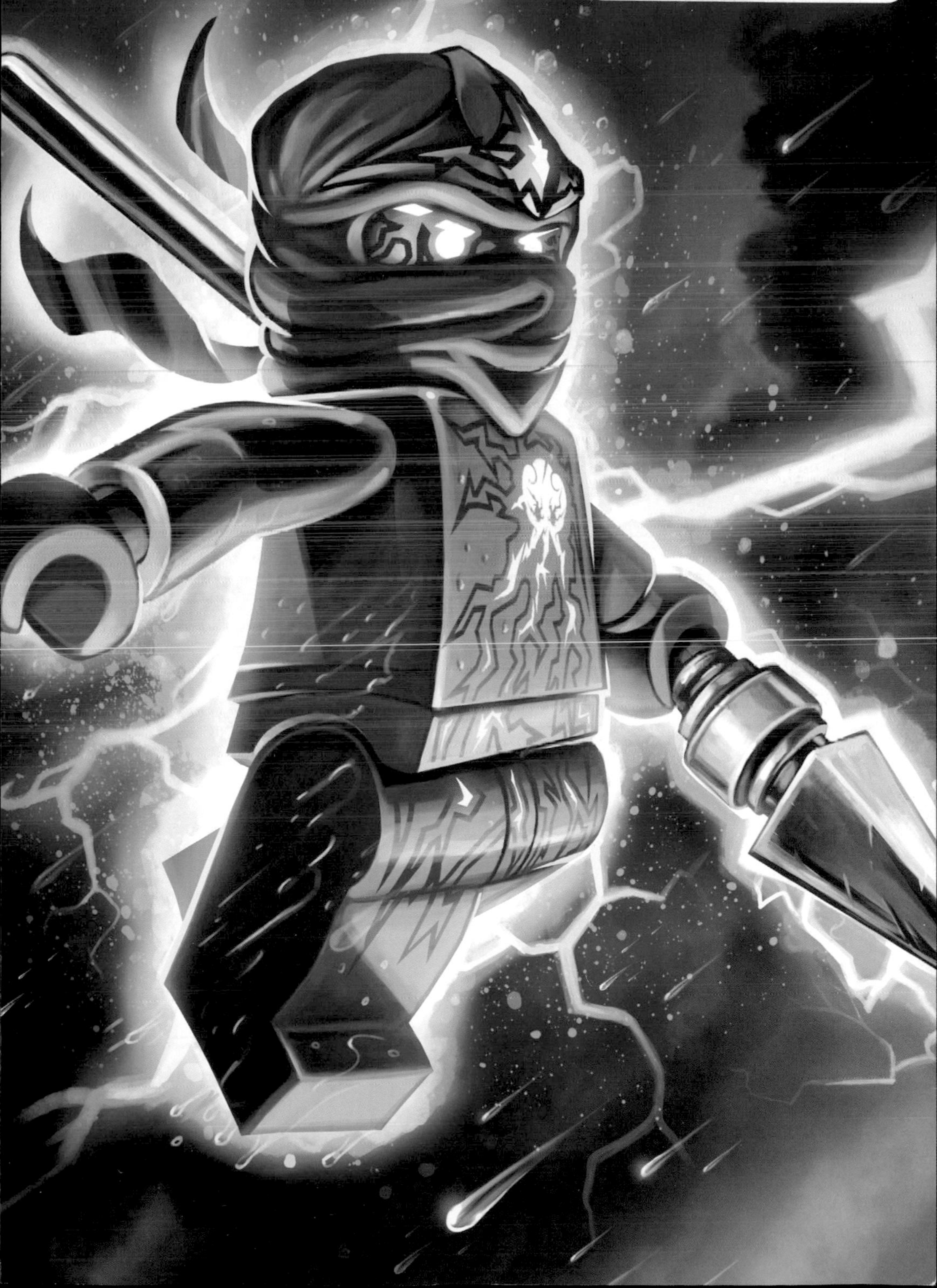

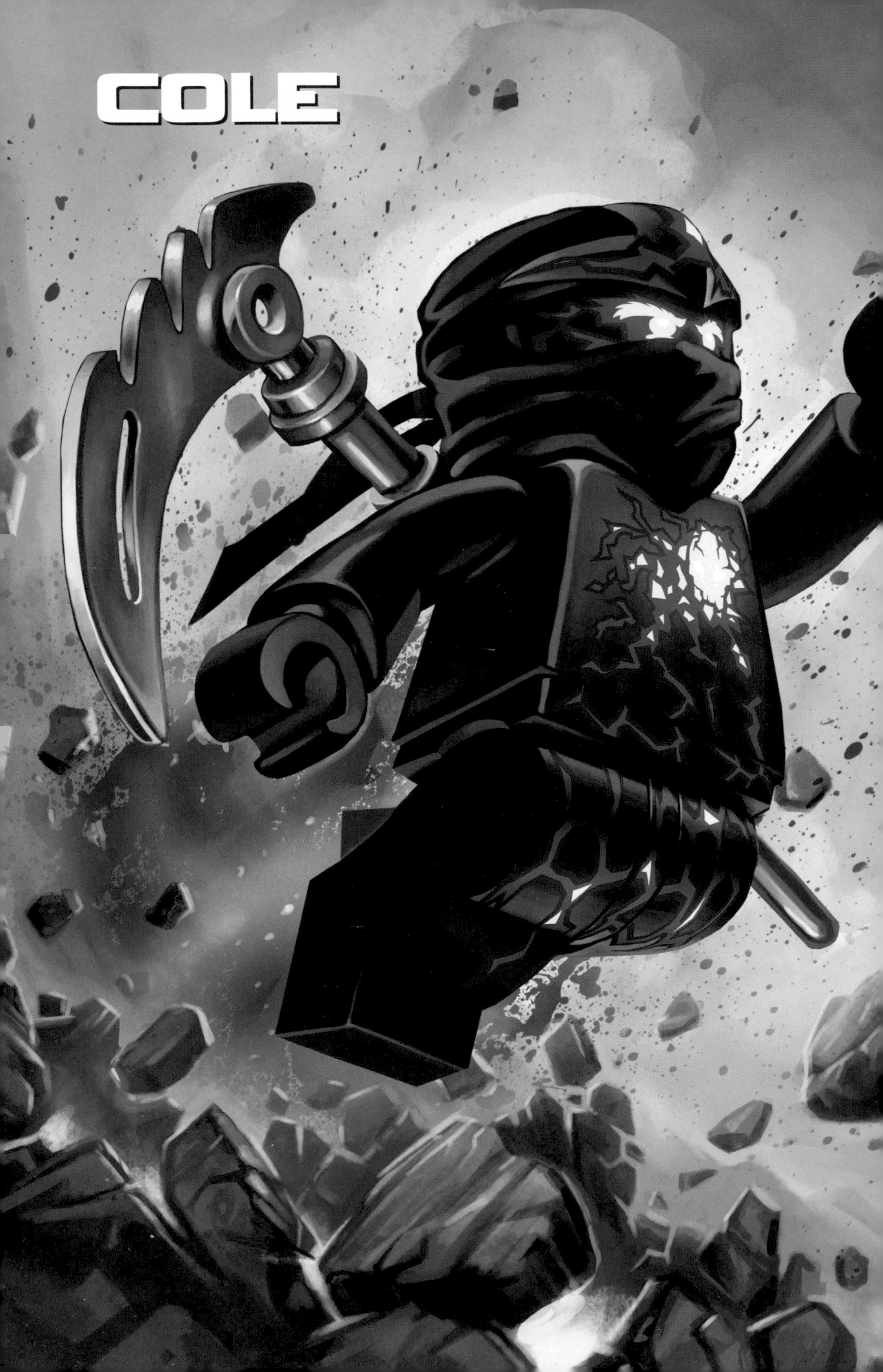
COLE

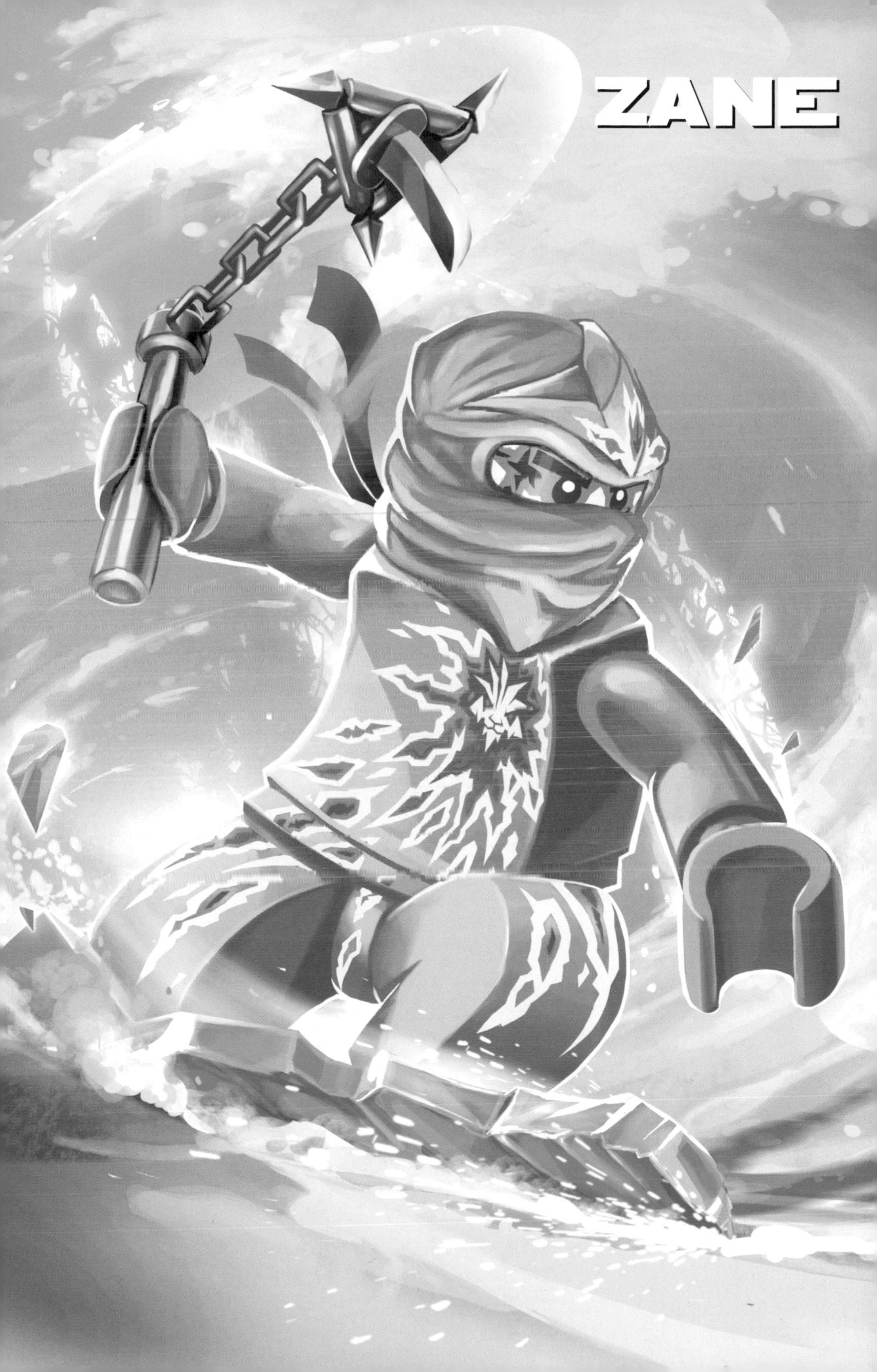
ZANE

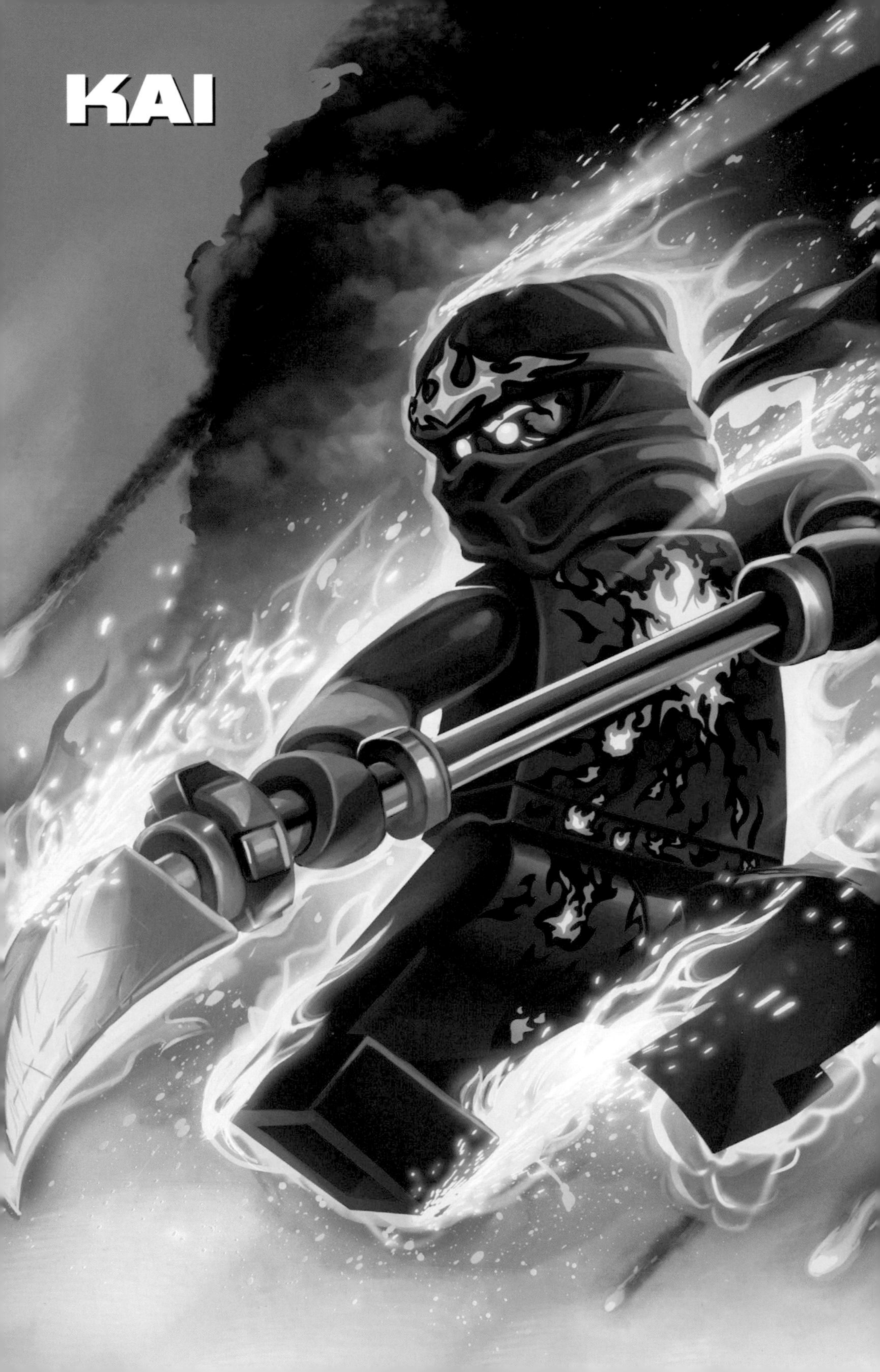
KAI

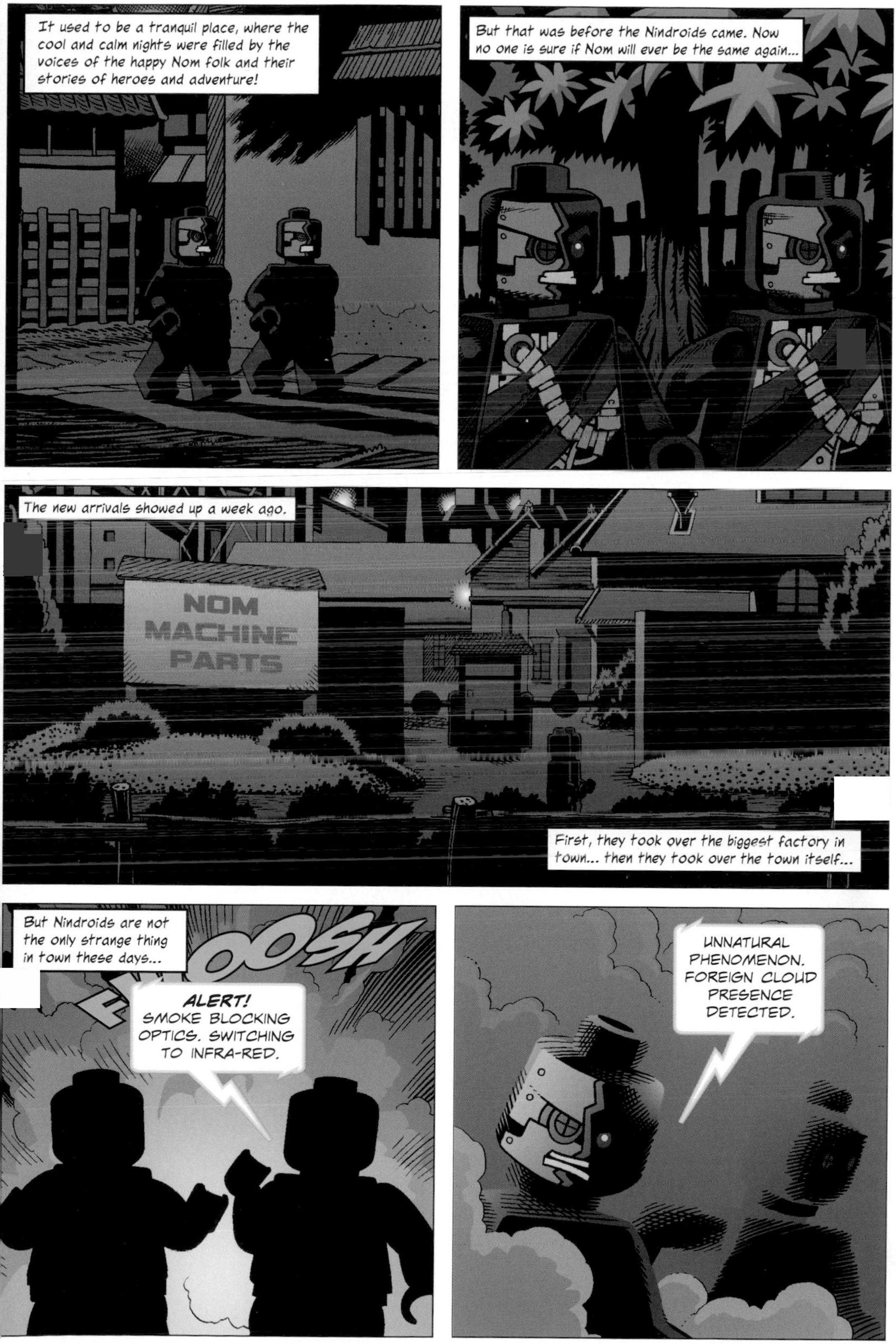

It used to be a tranquil place, where the cool and calm nights were filled by the voices of the happy Nom folk and their stories of heroes and adventure!
But that was before the Nindroids came. Now no one is sure if Nom will ever be the same again...
The new arrivals showed up a week ago.
NOM MACHINE PARTS
First, they took over the biggest factory in town... then they took over the town itself...
But Nindroids are not the only strange thing in town these days...
ALERT! SMOKE BLOCKING OPTICS. SWITCHING TO INFRA-RED.
UNNATURAL PHENOMENON. FOREIGN CLOUD PRESENCE DETECTED.

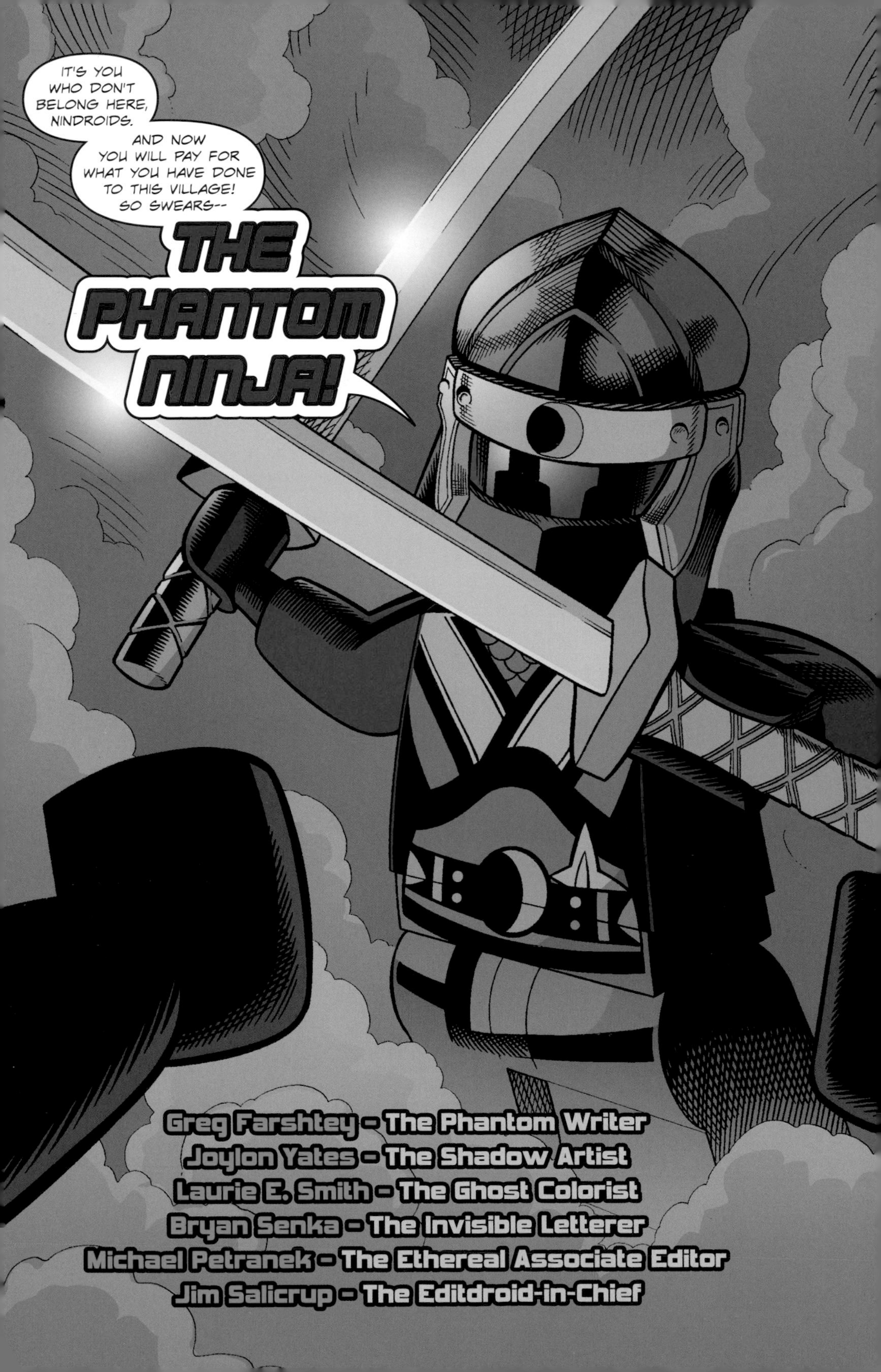
IT'S YOU WHO DON'T BELONG HERE, NINDROIDS.
AND NOW YOU WILL PAY FOR WHAT YOU HAVE DONE TO THIS VILLAGE! SO SWEARS--
THE PHANTOM NINJA!
Greg Farshtey - The Phantom Writer
Joylon Yates - The Shadow Artist
Laurie E. Smith - The Ghost Colorist
Bryan Senka - The Invisible Letterer
Michael Petranek - The Ethereal Associate Editor
Jim Salicrup - The Editdroid-in-Chief

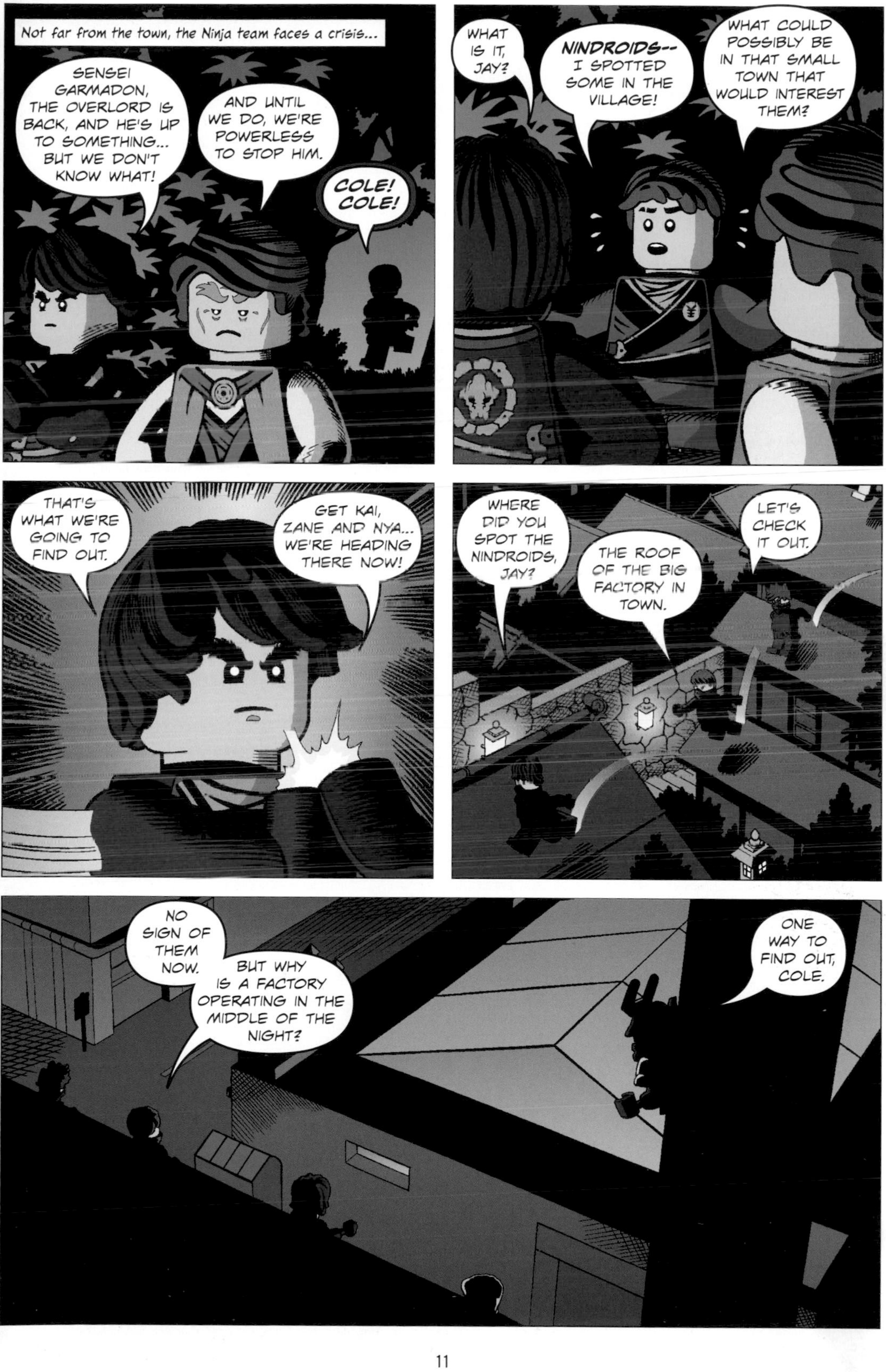

Not far from the town, the Ninja team faces a crisis...
SENSEI GARMADON, THE OVERLORD IS BACK, AND HE'S UP TO SOMETHING... BUT WE DON'T KNOW WHAT!
AND UNTIL WE DO, WE'RE POWERLESS TO STOP HIM.
COLE! COLE!
WHAT IS IT, JAY?
NINDROIDS-- I SPOTTED SOME IN THE VILLAGE!
WHAT COULD POSSIBLY BE IN THAT SMALL TOWN THAT WOULD INTEREST THEM?
THAT'S WHAT WE'RE GOING TO FIND OUT.
GET KAI, ZANE AND NYA... WE'RE HEADING THERE NOW!
WHERE DID YOU SPOT THE NINDROIDS, JAY?
THE ROOF OF THE BIG FACTORY IN TOWN.
LET'S CHECK IT OUT.
NO SIGN OF THEM NOW.
BUT WHY IS A FACTORY OPERATING IN THE MIDDLE OF THE NIGHT?
ONE WAY TO FIND OUT, COLE.

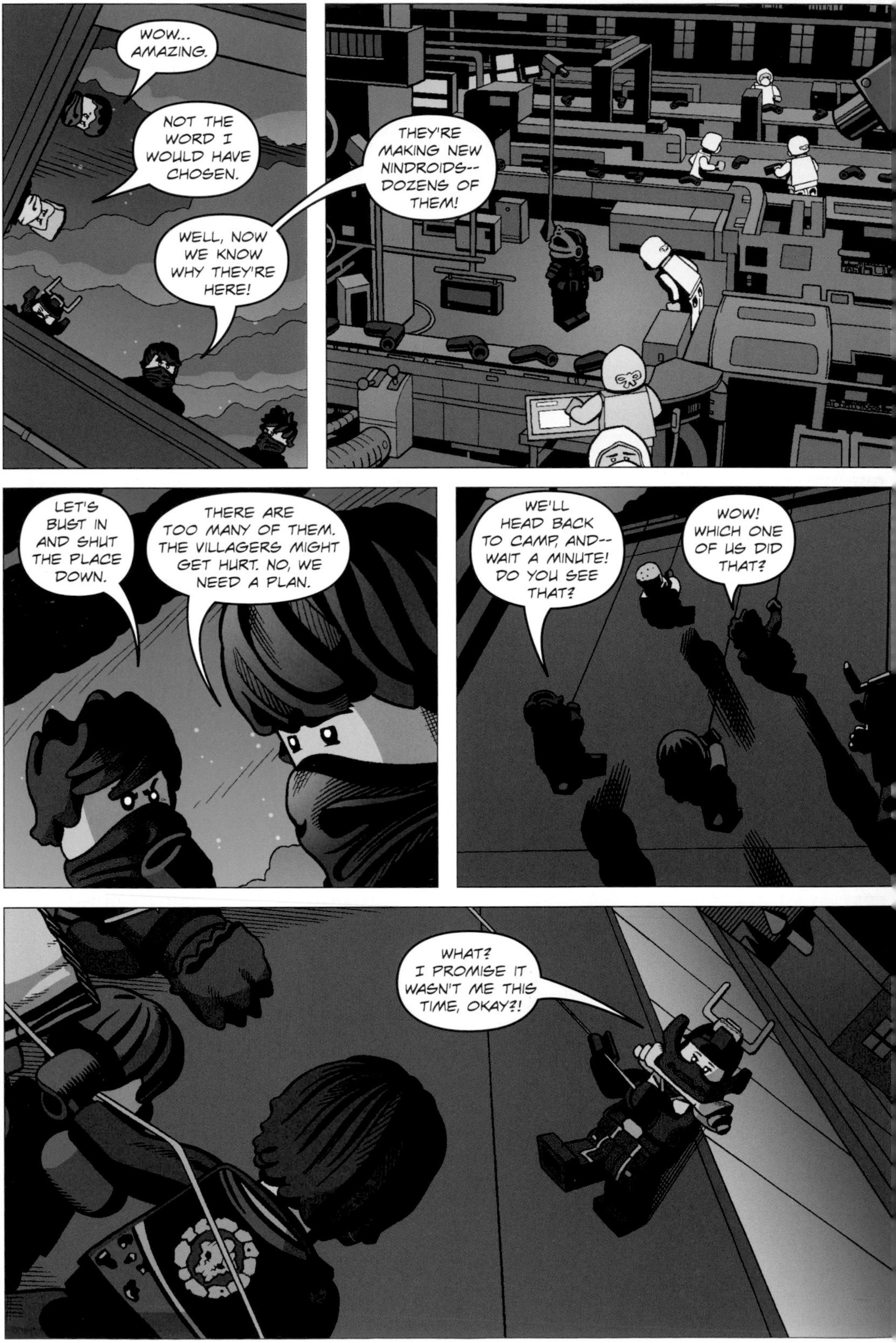
WOW... AMAZING.
NOT THE WORD I WOULD HAVE CHOSEN.
WELL, NOW WE KNOW WHY THEY'RE HERE!
THEY'RE MAKING NEW NINDROIDS-- DOZENS OF THEM!
LET'S BUST IN AND SHUT THE PLACE DOWN.
THERE ARE TOO MANY OF THEM. THE VILLAGERS MIGHT GET HURT. NO, WE NEED A PLAN.
WE'LL HEAD BACK TO CAMP, AND-- WAIT A MINUTE! DO YOU SEE THAT?
WOW! WHICH ONE OF US DID THAT?
WHAT? I PROMISE IT WASN'T ME THIS TIME, OKAY?!

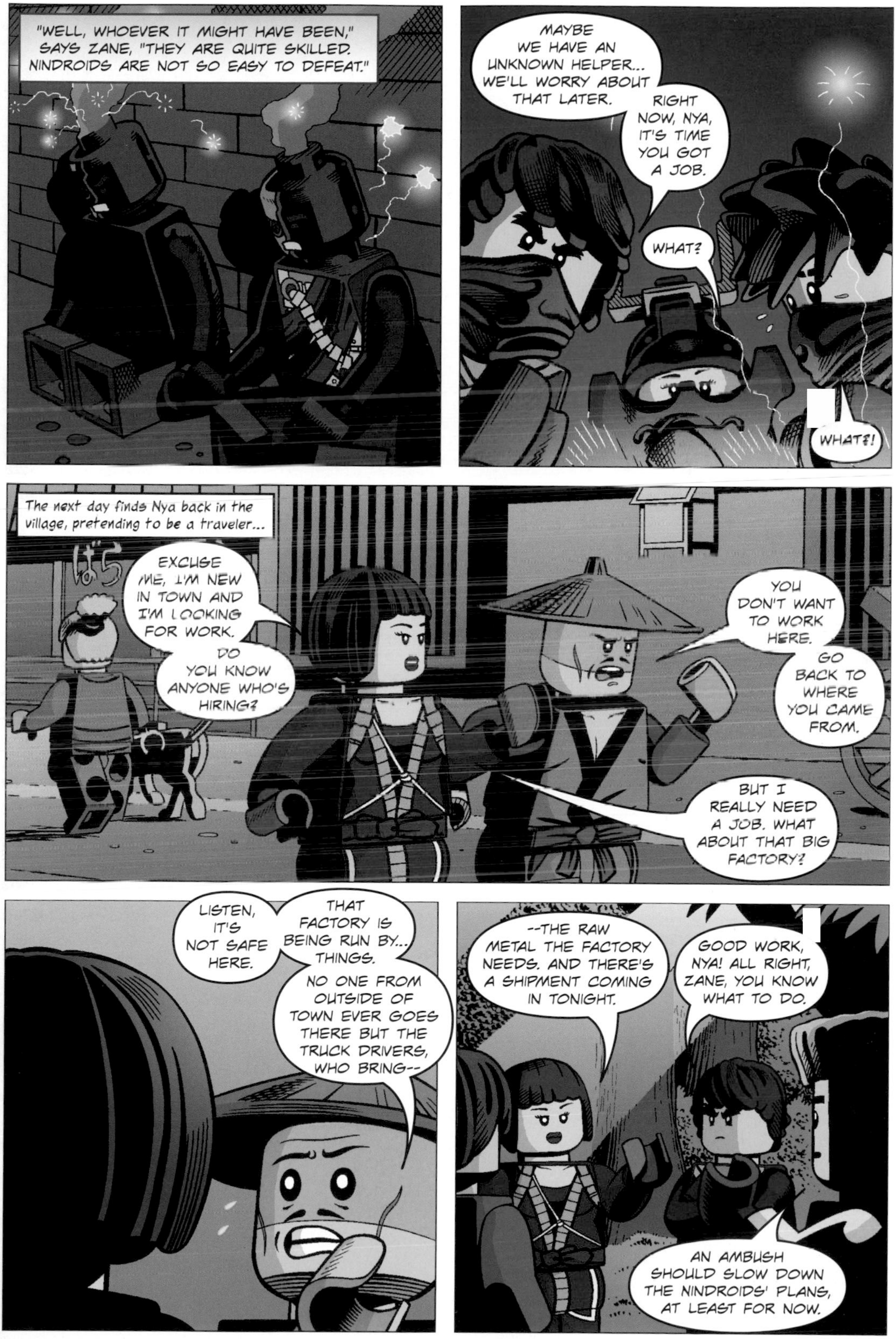
"WELL, WHOEVER IT MIGHT HAVE BEEN," SAYS ZANE, "THEY ARE QUITE SKILLED. NINDROIDS ARE NOT SO EASY TO DEFEAT."
MAYBE WE HAVE AN UNKNOWN HELPER... WE'LL WORRY ABOUT THAT LATER.
RIGHT NOW, NYA, IT'S TIME YOU GOT A JOB.
WHAT?
WHAT?!
The next day finds Nya back in the village, pretending to be a traveler...
EXCUSE ME, I'M NEW IN TOWN AND I'M LOOKING FOR WORK.
DO YOU KNOW ANYONE WHO'S HIRING?
YOU DON'T WANT TO WORK HERE.
GO BACK TO WHERE YOU CAME FROM.
BUT I REALLY NEED A JOB. WHAT ABOUT THAT BIG FACTORY?
LISTEN, IT'S NOT SAFE HERE.
THAT FACTORY IS BEING RUN BY... THINGS.
NO ONE FROM OUTSIDE OF TOWN EVER GOES THERE BUT THE TRUCK DRIVERS, WHO BRING--
--THE RAW METAL THE FACTORY NEEDS. AND THERE'S A SHIPMENT COMING IN TONIGHT.
GOOD WORK, NYA! ALL RIGHT, ZANE, YOU KNOW WHAT TO DO.
AN AMBUSH SHOULD SLOW DOWN THE NINDROIDS' PLANS, AT LEAST FOR NOW.

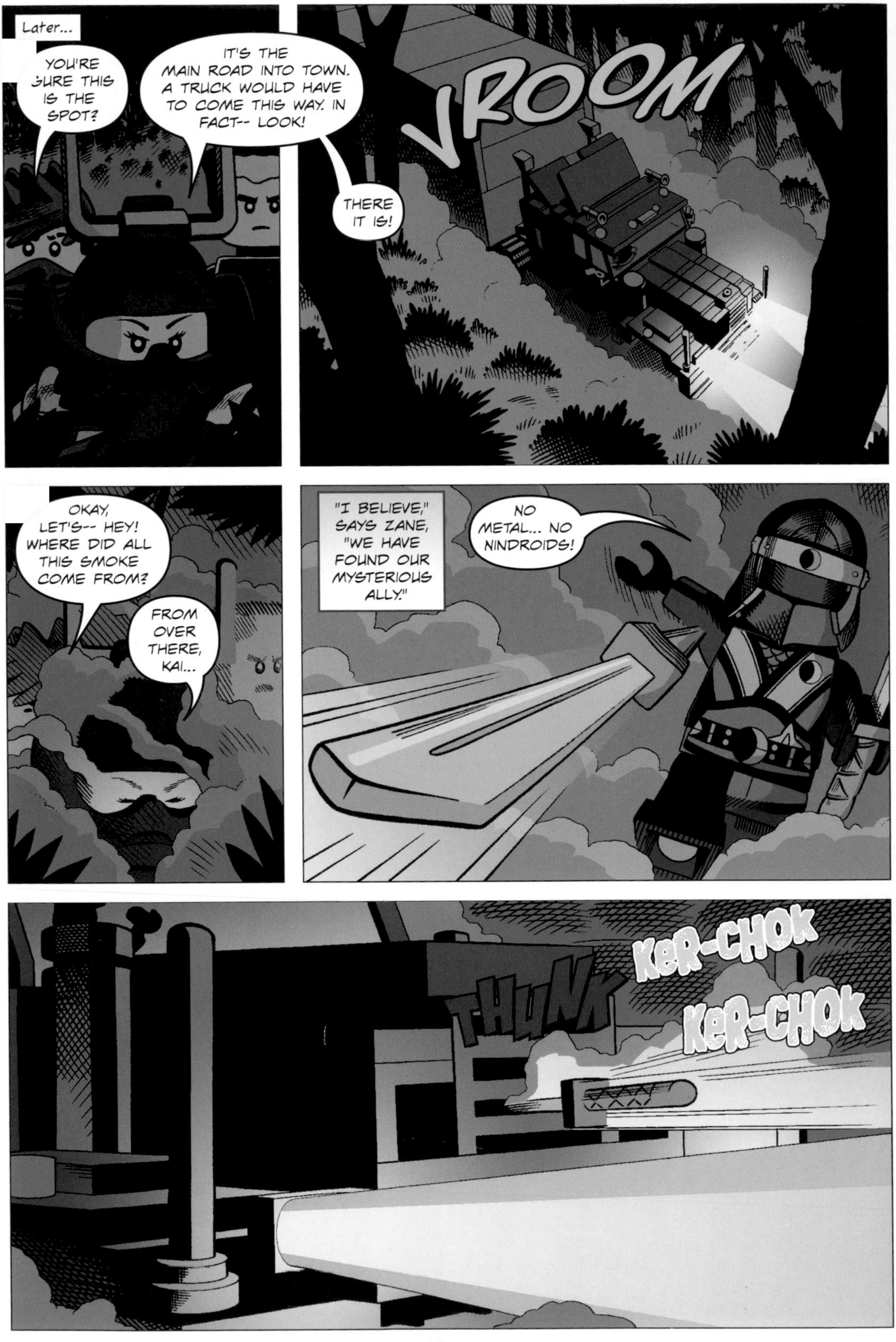
Later...
YOU'RE SURE THIS IS THE SPOT?
IT'S THE MAIN ROAD INTO TOWN. A TRUCK WOULD HAVE TO COME THIS WAY. IN FACT-- LOOK!
THERE IT IS!
VROOM
OKAY, LET'S-- HEY! WHERE DID ALL THIS SMOKE COME FROM?
FROM OVER THERE, KAI...
"I BELIEVE," SAYS ZANE, "WE HAVE FOUND OUR MYSTERIOUS ALLY."
NO METAL... NO NINDROIDS!
THUNK
KER-CHOK
KER-CHOK

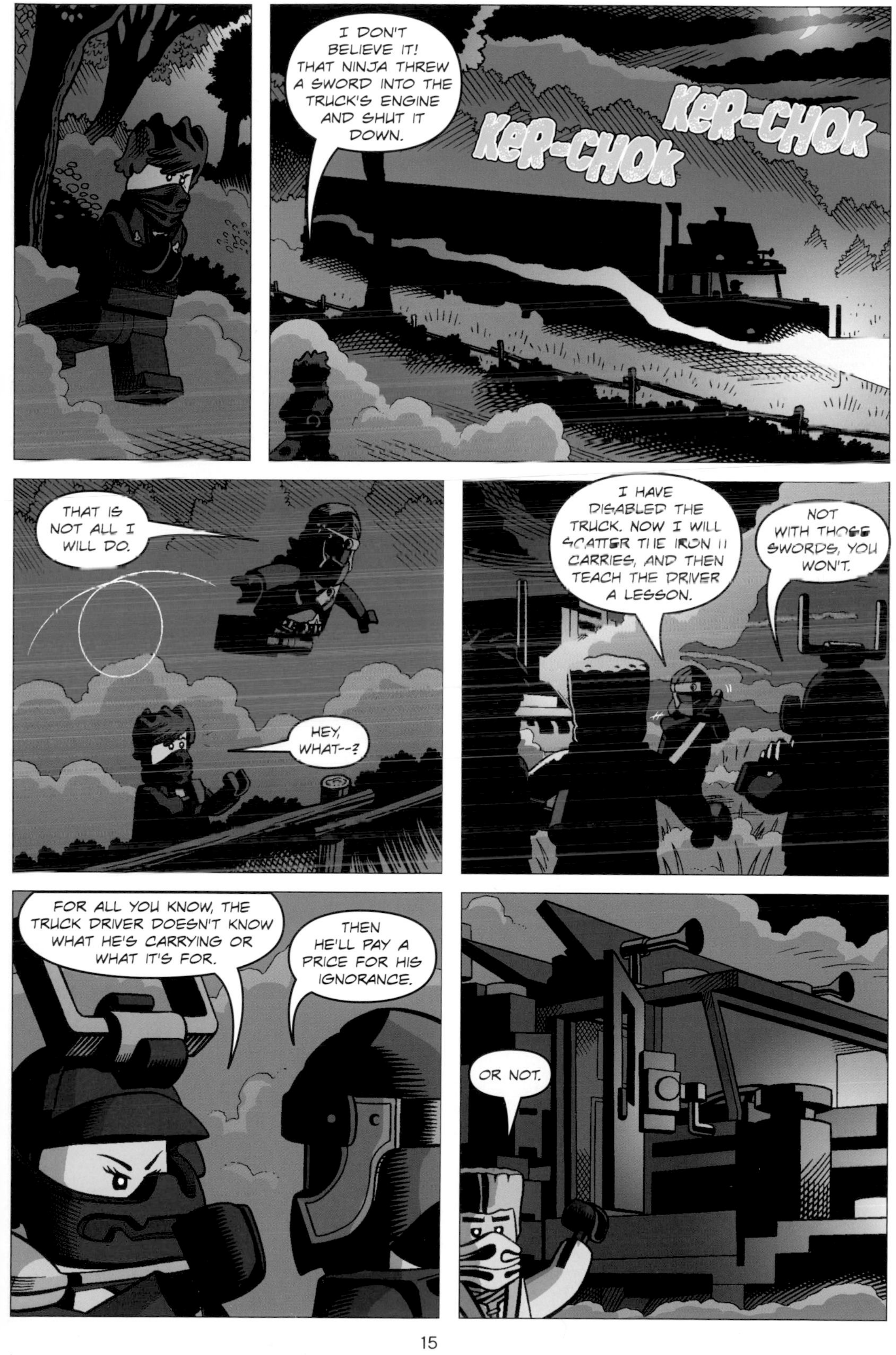
I DON'T BELIEVE IT! THAT NINJA THREW A SWORD INTO THE TRUCK'S ENGINE AND SHUT IT DOWN.
KER-CHOK
KER-CHOK
THAT IS NOT ALL I WILL DO.
HEY, WHAT--?
I HAVE DISABLED THE TRUCK. NOW I WILL SCATTER THE IRON IT CARRIES, AND THEN TEACH THE DRIVER A LESSON.
NOT WITH THOSE SWORDS, YOU WON'T.
FOR ALL YOU KNOW, THE TRUCK DRIVER DOESN'T KNOW WHAT HE'S CARRYING OR WHAT IT'S FOR.
THEN HE'LL PAY A PRICE FOR HIS IGNORANCE.
OR NOT.

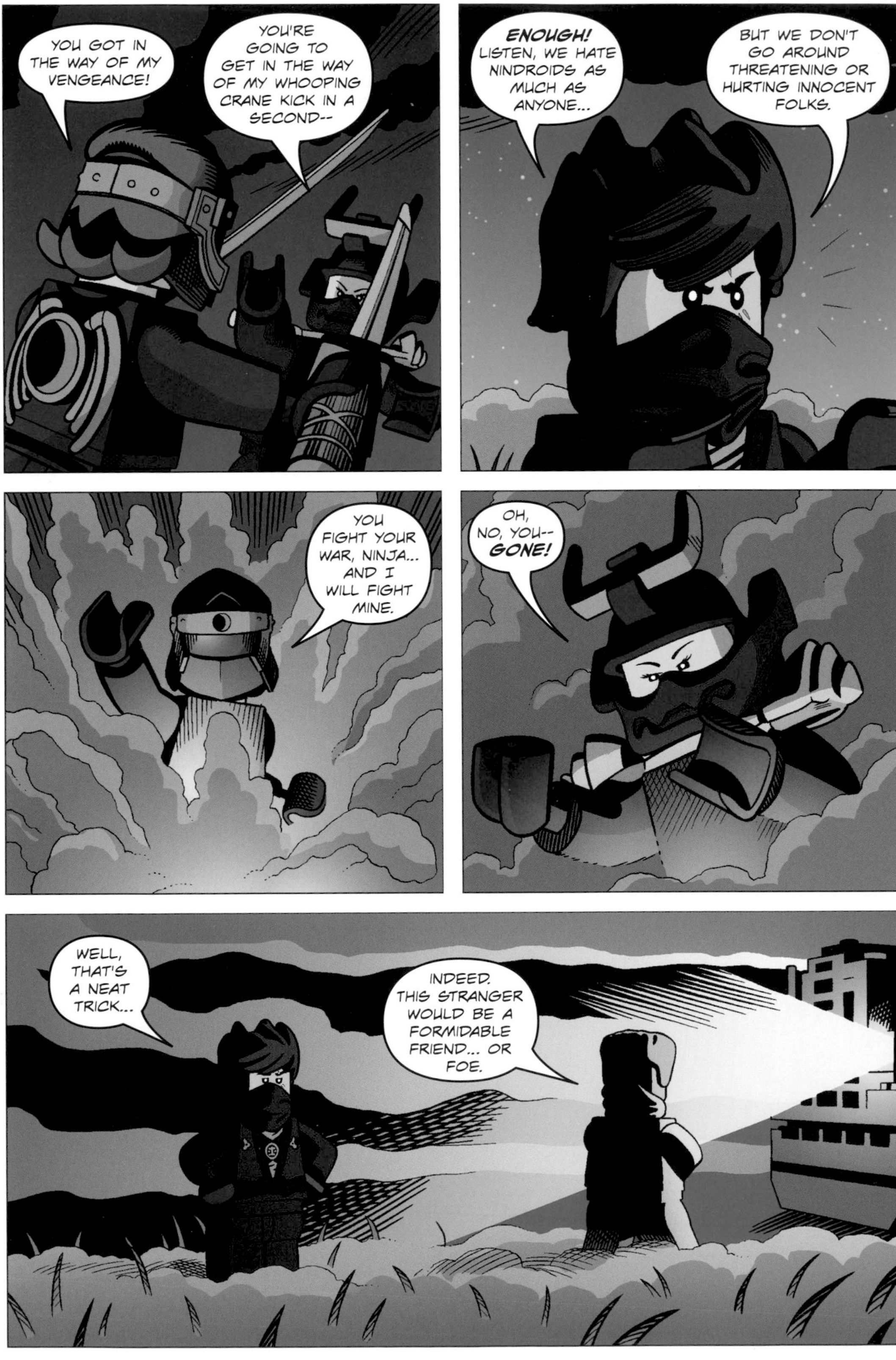
YOU GOT IN THE WAY OF MY VENGEANCE!
YOU'RE GOING TO GET IN THE WAY OF MY WHOOPING CRANE KICK IN A SECOND--
ENOUGH! LISTEN, WE HATE NINDROIDS AS MUCH AS ANYONE...
BUT WE DON'T GO AROUND THREATENING OR HURTING INNOCENT FOLKS.
YOU FIGHT YOUR WAR, NINJA... AND I WILL FIGHT MINE.
OH, NO, YOU-- **GONE!**
WELL, THAT'S A NEAT TRICK...
INDEED. THIS STRANGER WOULD BE A FORMIDABLE FRIEND... OR FOE.

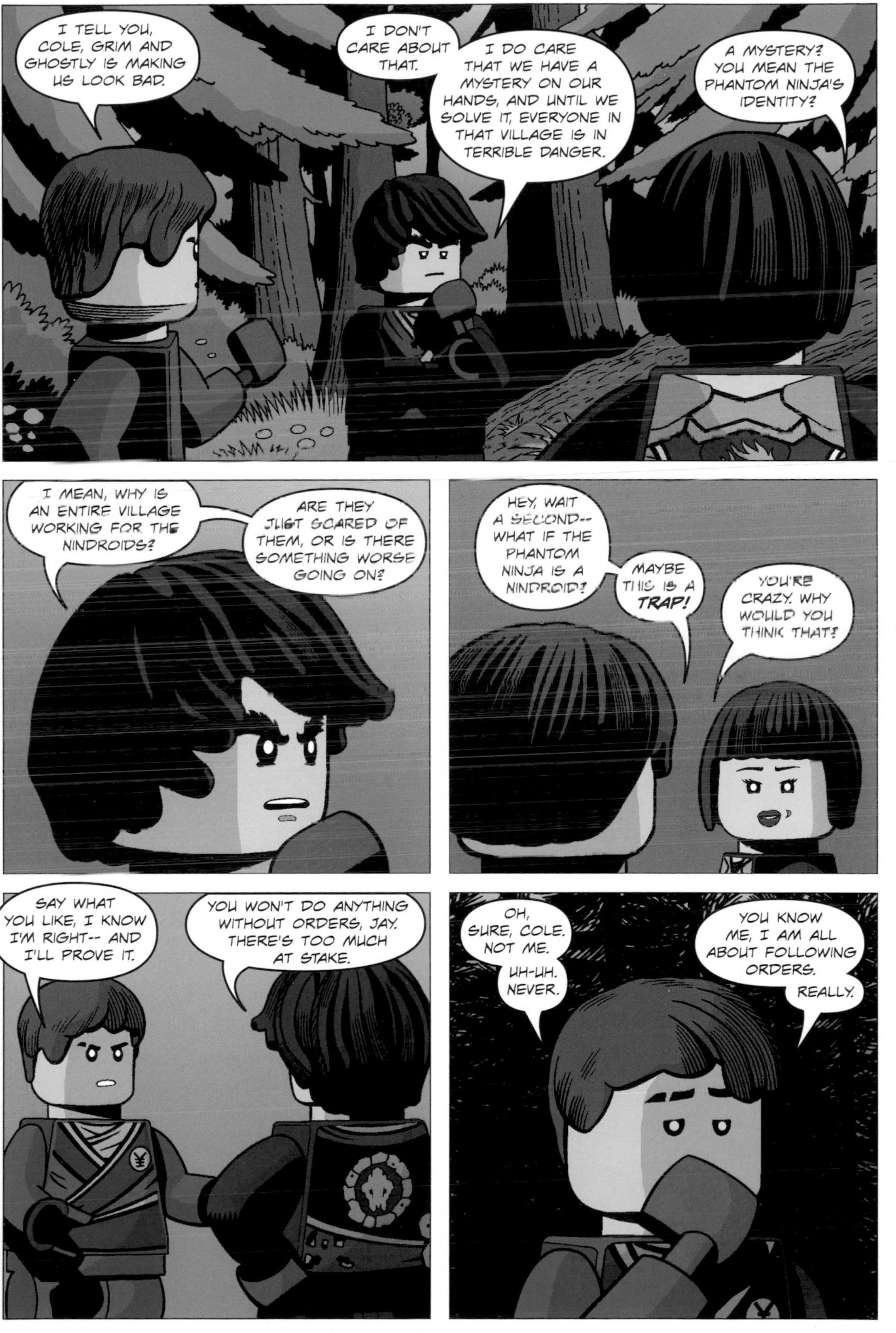
I TELL YOU, COLE, GRIM AND GHOSTLY IS MAKING US LOOK BAD.
I DON'T CARE ABOUT THAT.
I DO CARE THAT WE HAVE A MYSTERY ON OUR HANDS, AND UNTIL WE SOLVE IT, EVERYONE IN THAT VILLAGE IS IN TERRIBLE DANGER.
A MYSTERY? YOU MEAN THE PHANTOM NINJA'S IDENTITY?
I MEAN, WHY IS AN ENTIRE VILLAGE WORKING FOR THE NINDROIDS?
ARE THEY JUST SCARED OF THEM, OR IS THERE SOMETHING WORSE GOING ON?
HEY, WAIT A SECOND-- WHAT IF THE PHANTOM NINJA IS A NINDROID?
MAYBE THIS IS A TRAP!
YOU'RE CRAZY. WHY WOULD YOU THINK THAT?
SAY WHAT YOU LIKE, I KNOW I'M RIGHT-- AND I'LL PROVE IT.
YOU WON'T DO ANYTHING WITHOUT ORDERS, JAY. THERE'S TOO MUCH AT STAKE.
OH, SURE, COLE. NOT ME.
UH-UH. NEVER.
YOU KNOW ME, I AM ALL ABOUT FOLLOWING ORDERS.
REALLY.

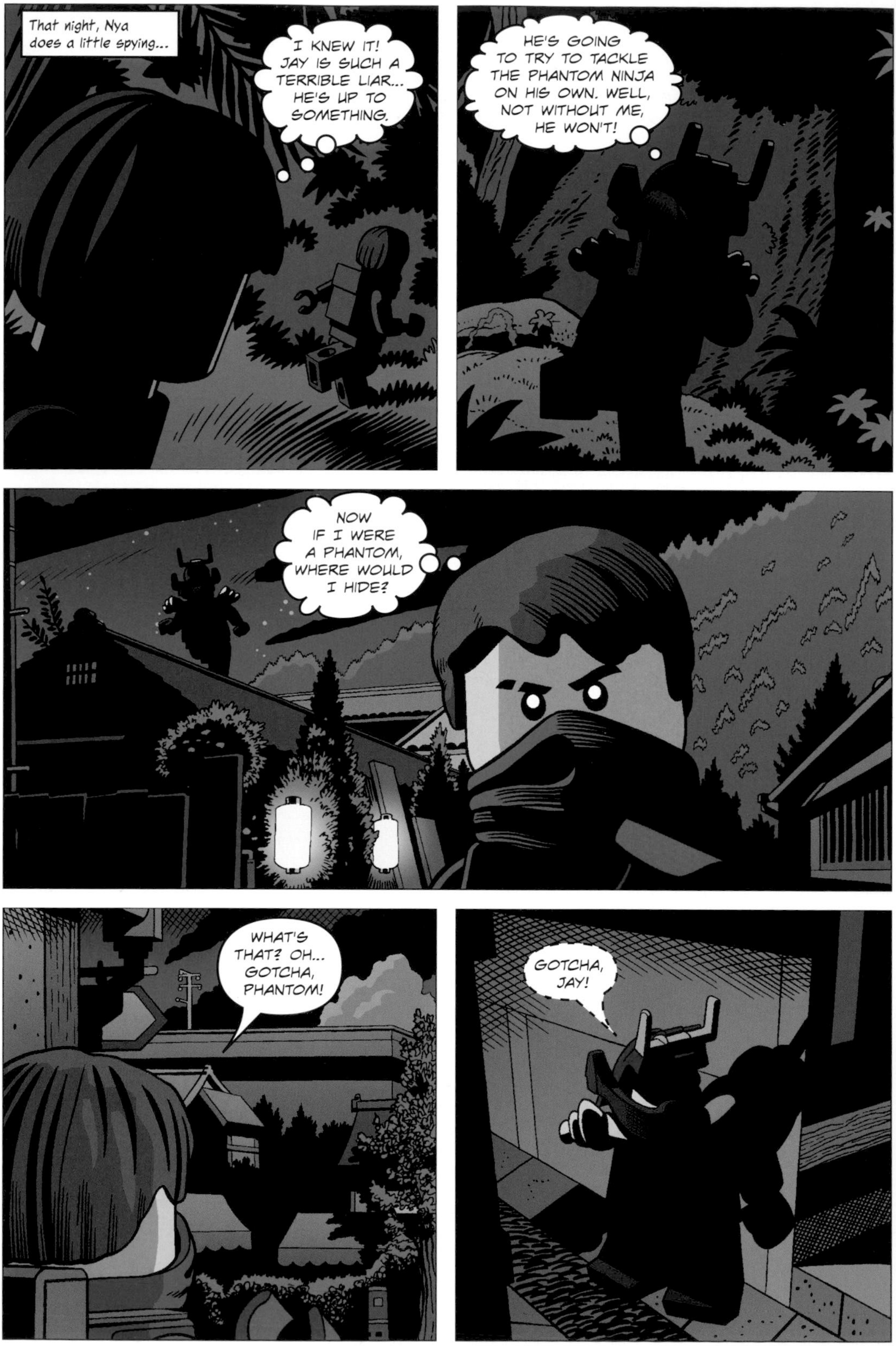
That night, Nya does a little spying...
I KNEW IT! JAY IS SUCH A TERRIBLE LIAR... HE'S UP TO SOMETHING.
HE'S GOING TO TRY TO TACKLE THE PHANTOM NINJA ON HIS OWN. WELL, NOT WITHOUT ME, HE WON'T!
NOW IF I WERE A PHANTOM, WHERE WOULD I HIDE?
WHAT'S THAT? OH... GOTCHA, PHANTOM!
GOTCHA, JAY!

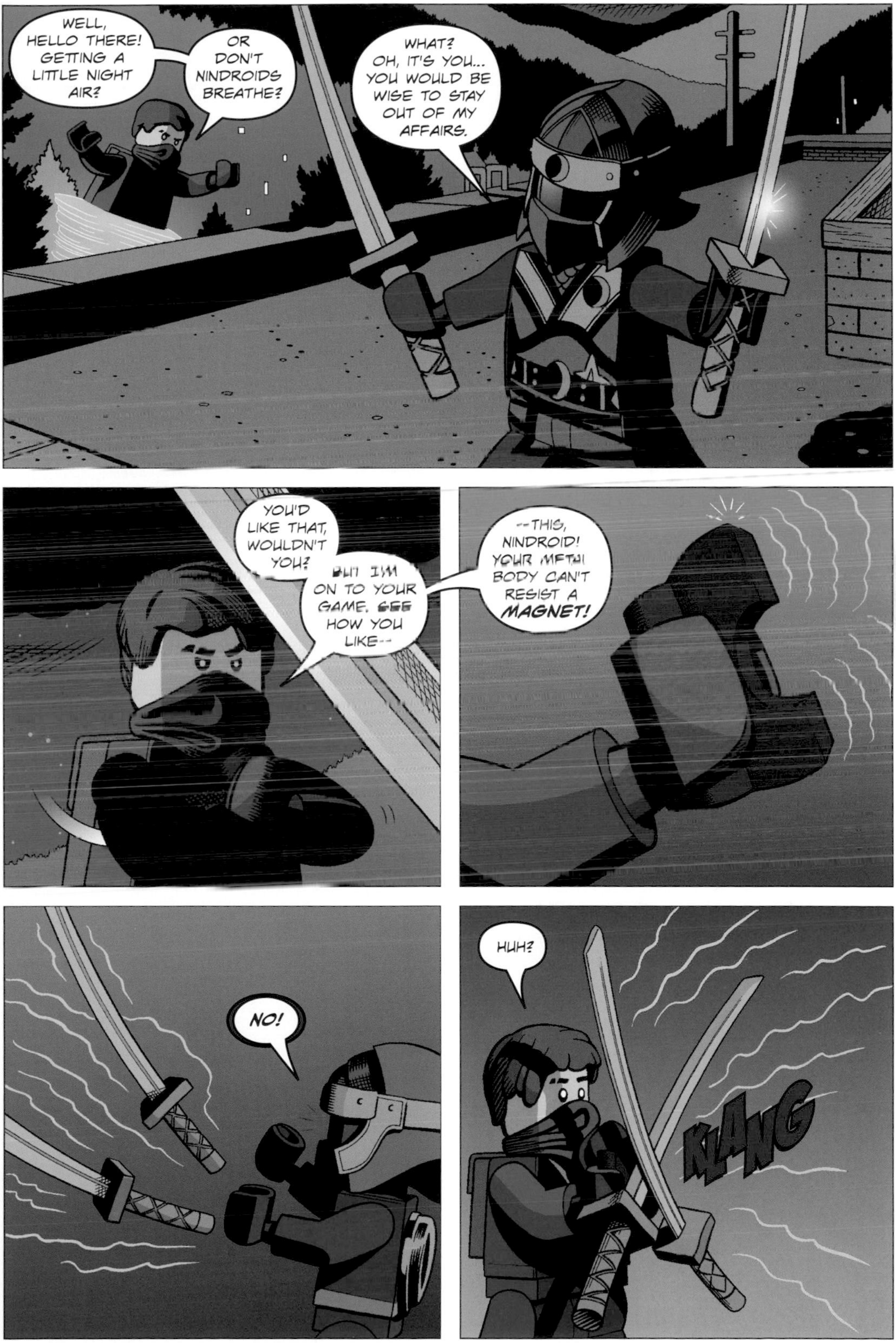
WELL, HELLO THERE! GETTING A LITTLE NIGHT AIR?
OR DON'T NINDROIDS BREATHE?
WHAT? OH, IT'S YOU... YOU WOULD BE WISE TO STAY OUT OF MY AFFAIRS.
YOU'D LIKE THAT, WOULDN'T YOU?
BUT I'M ON TO YOUR GAME. SEE HOW YOU LIKE--
--THIS, NINDROID! YOUR METAL BODY CAN'T RESIST A *MAGNET!*
NO!
HUH?
KLANG

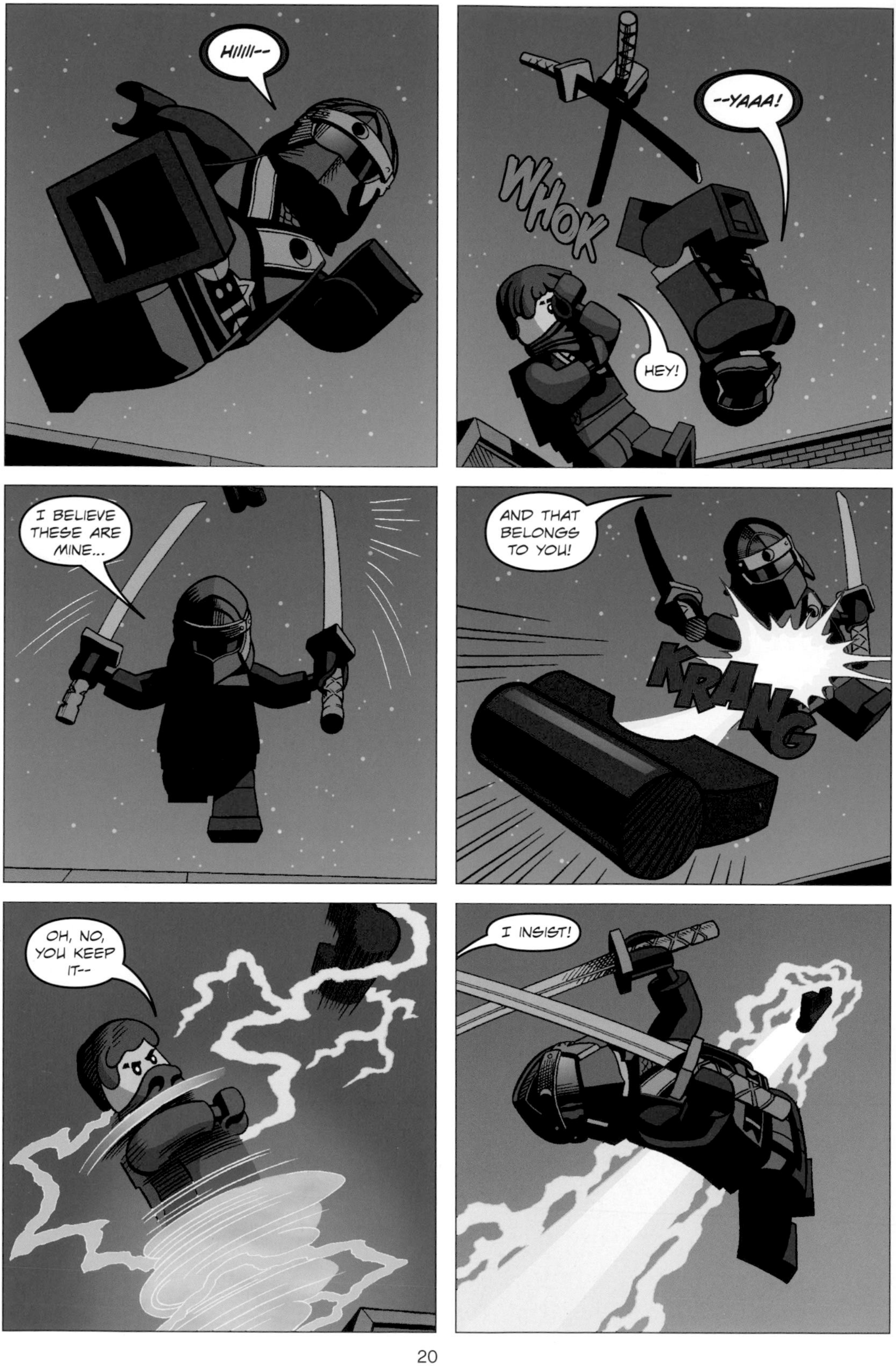
HIIIII--
--YAAA!
WHOK
HEY!
I BELIEVE THESE ARE MINE...
AND THAT BELONGS TO YOU!
KRANG
OH, NO, YOU KEEP IT--
I INSIST!

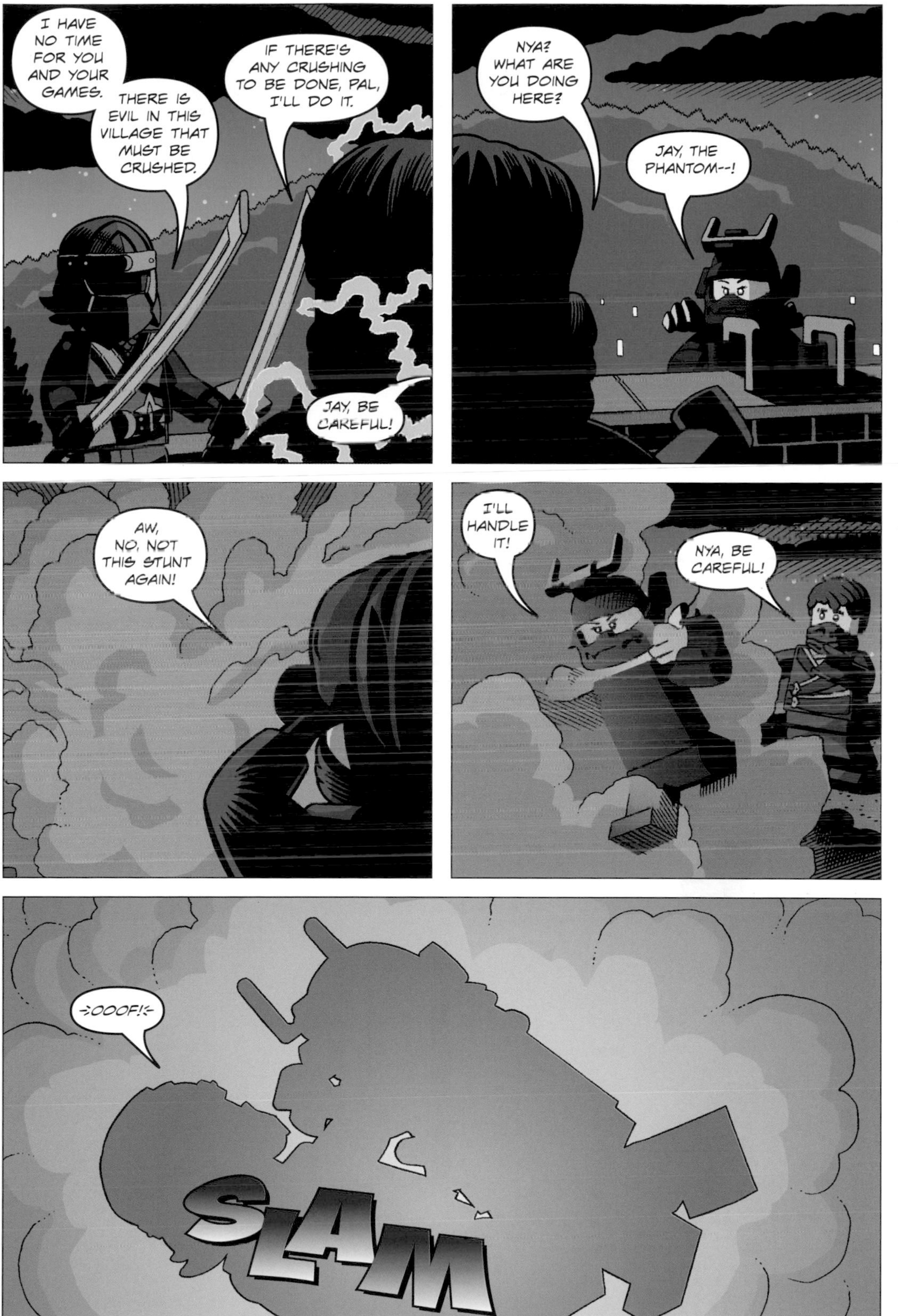
I HAVE NO TIME FOR YOU AND YOUR GAMES.
THERE IS EVIL IN THIS VILLAGE THAT MUST BE CRUSHED.
IF THERE'S ANY CRUSHING TO BE DONE, PAL, I'LL DO IT.
JAY, BE CAREFUL!
NYA? WHAT ARE YOU DOING HERE?
JAY, THE PHANTOM--!
AW, NO, NOT THIS STUNT AGAIN!
I'LL HANDLE IT!
NYA, BE CAREFUL!
OOOF!
SLAM

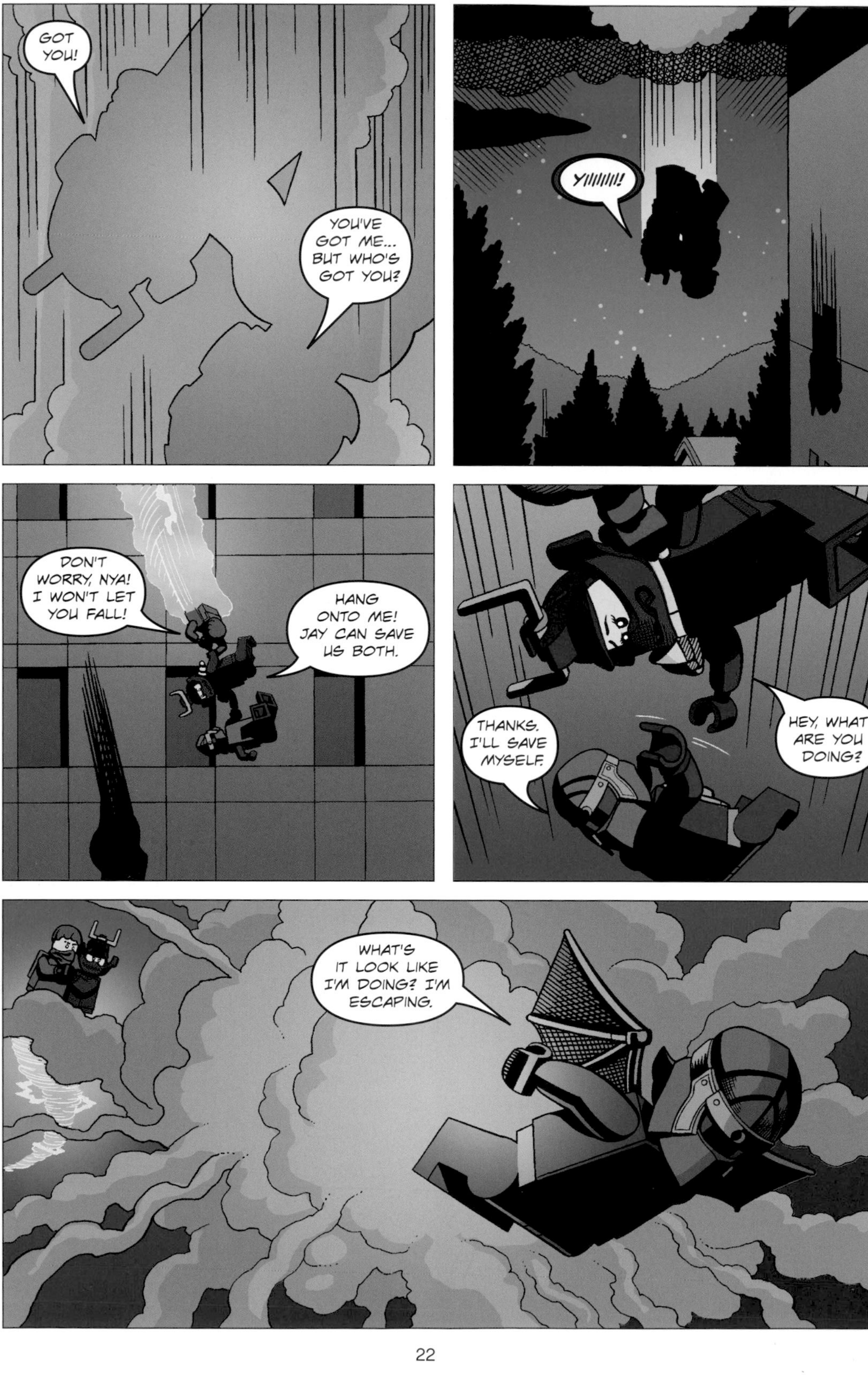
GOT YOU!
YOU'VE GOT ME... BUT WHO'S GOT YOU?
YIIIIIII!
DON'T WORRY, NYA! I WON'T LET YOU FALL!
HANG ONTO ME! JAY CAN SAVE US BOTH.
THANKS. I'LL SAVE MYSELF.
HEY, WHAT ARE YOU DOING?
WHAT'S IT LOOK LIKE I'M DOING? I'M ESCAPING.

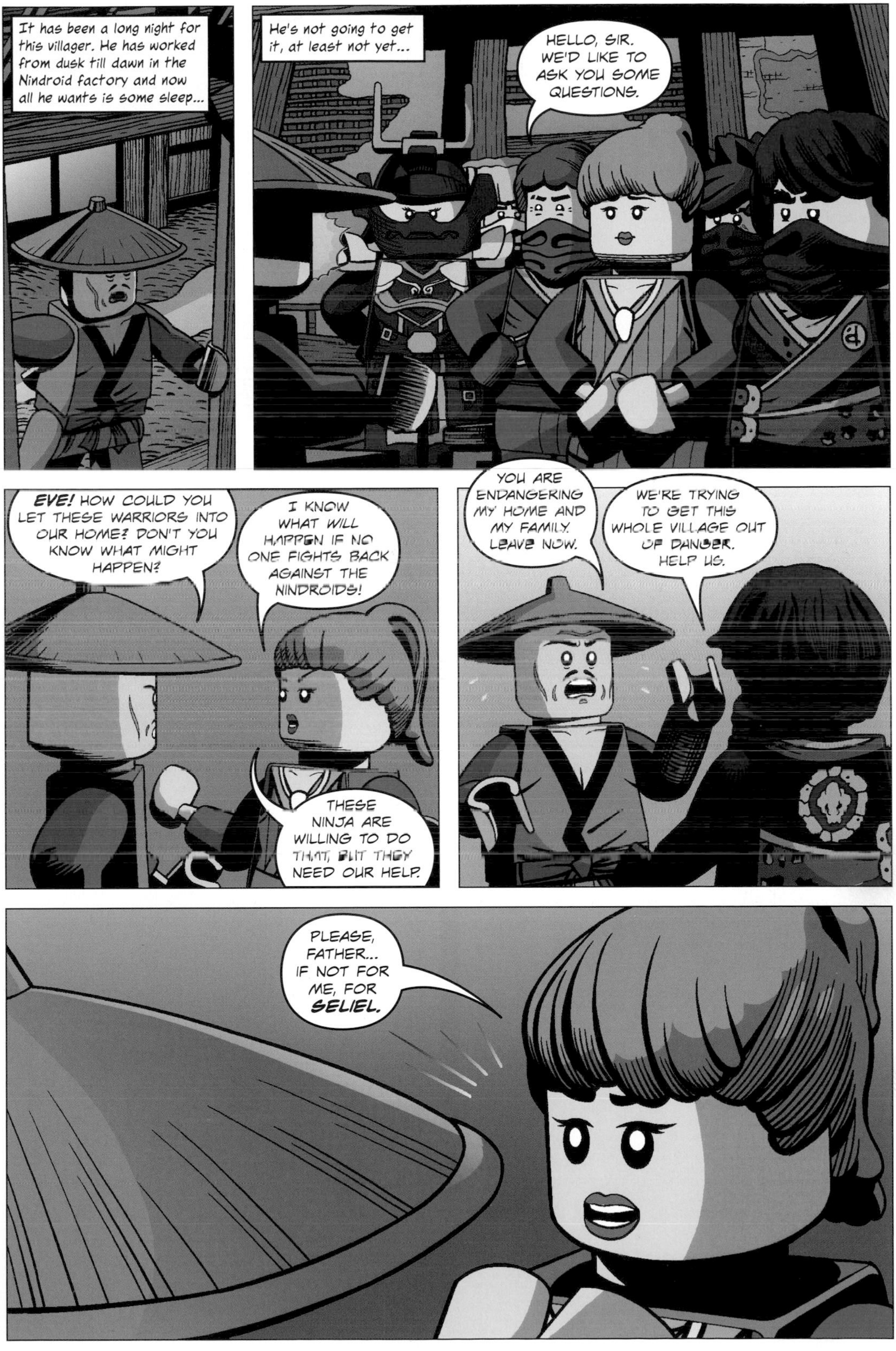
It has been a long night for this villager. He has worked from dusk till dawn in the Nindroid factory and now all he wants is some sleep...
He's not going to get it, at least not yet...
HELLO, SIR. WE'D LIKE TO ASK YOU SOME QUESTIONS.
EVE! HOW COULD YOU LET THESE WARRIORS INTO OUR HOME? DON'T YOU KNOW WHAT MIGHT HAPPEN?
I KNOW WHAT WILL HAPPEN IF NO ONE FIGHTS BACK AGAINST THE NINDROIDS!
THESE NINJA ARE WILLING TO DO THAT, BUT THEY NEED OUR HELP.
YOU ARE ENDANGERING MY HOME AND MY FAMILY. LEAVE NOW.
WE'RE TRYING TO GET THIS WHOLE VILLAGE OUT OF DANGER. HELP US.
PLEASE, FATHER... IF NOT FOR ME, FOR SELIEL.

ALL RIGHT. I WILL TELL YOU WHAT I KNOW, AND THEN YOU MUST GO. PLEASE.

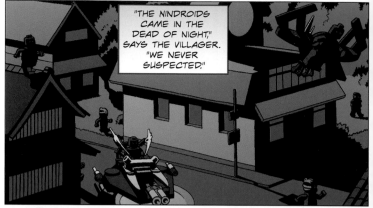

"THE NINDROIDS CAME IN THE DEAD OF NIGHT," SAYS THE VILLAGER. "WE NEVER SUSPECTED."

"IN THE MORNING, WE LEARNED THEY HAD TAKEN THE MAYOR AND HIS DAUGHTER, SELIEL, HOSTAGE. THE TWO OF THEM WOULD BE SAFE AS LONG AS WE OBEYED THE NINDROIDS."

"THEY PUT US TO WORK IN THE FACTORY, BUILDING PARTS TO CREATE MORE OF THEM. WE HAD NO CHOICE BUT TO DO WHAT WE WERE TOLD."

WE'RE GOING TO GIVE YOU THAT CHOICE. BUT, TELL ME, WHAT ABOUT THIS PHANTOM NINJA?

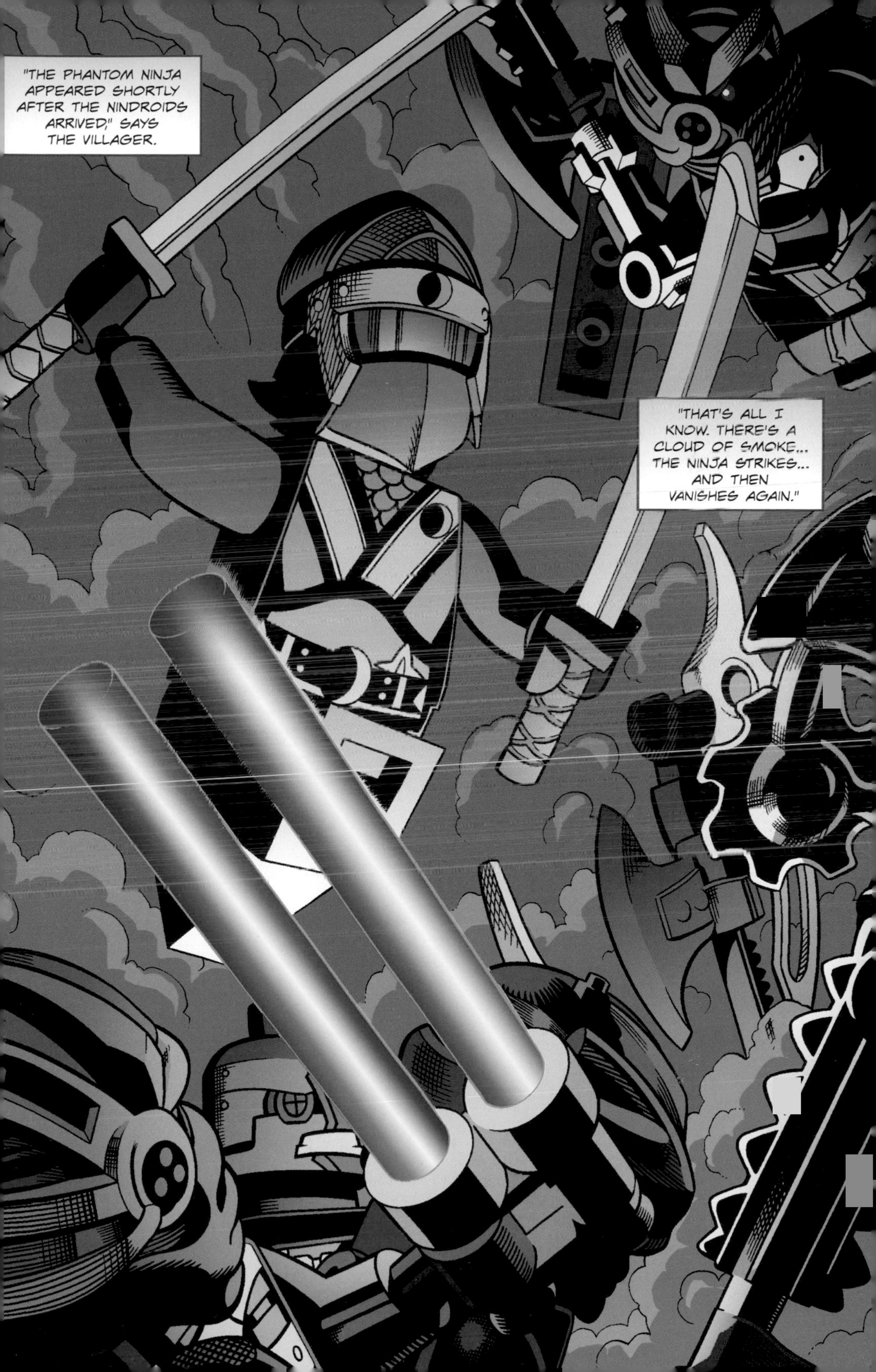
"THE PHANTOM NINJA APPEARED SHORTLY AFTER THE NINDROIDS ARRIVED," SAYS THE VILLAGER.
"THAT'S ALL I KNOW. THERE'S A CLOUD OF SMOKE... THE NINJA STRIKES... AND THEN VANISHES AGAIN."

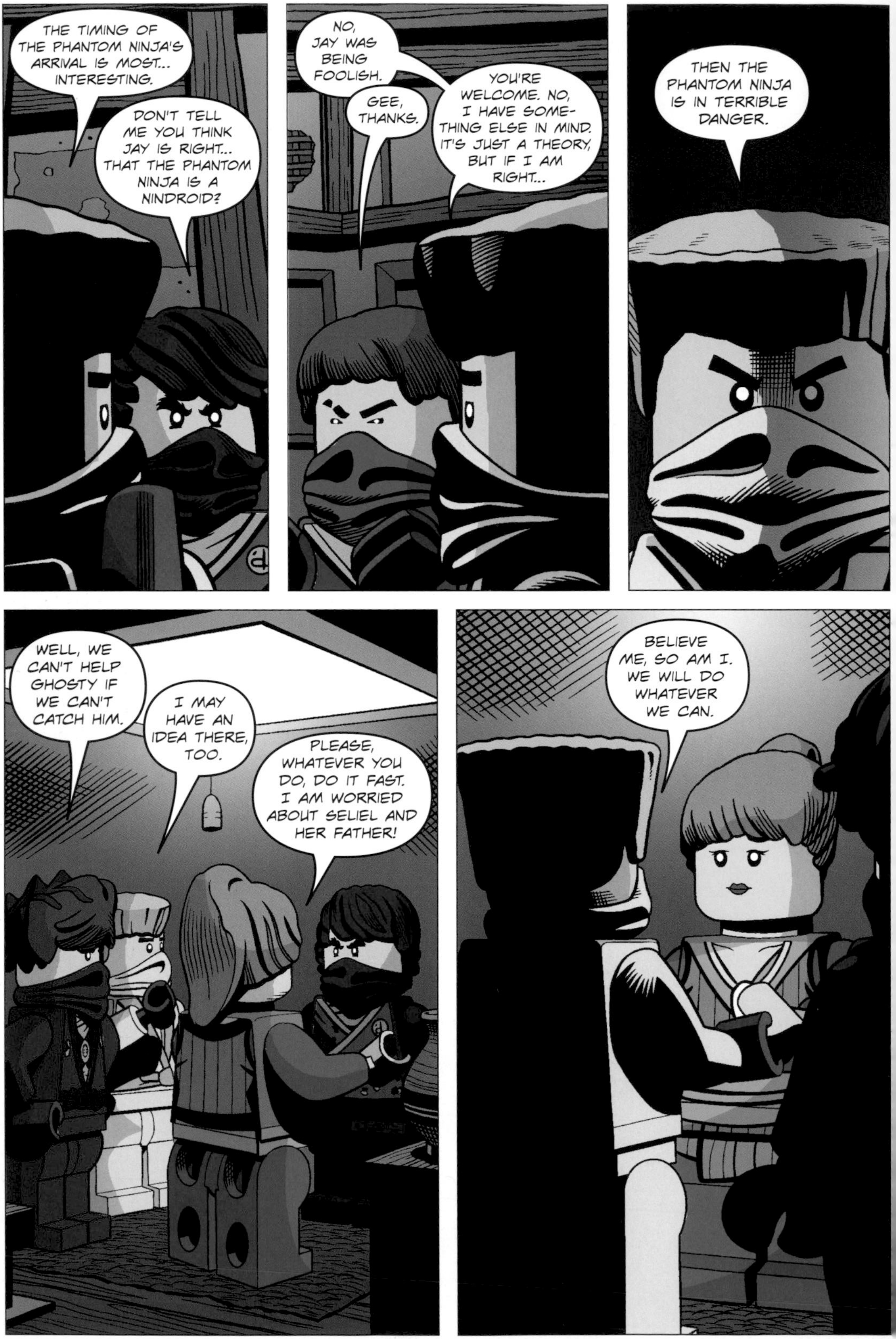
THE TIMING OF THE PHANTOM NINJA'S ARRIVAL IS MOST... INTERESTING.
DON'T TELL ME YOU THINK JAY IS RIGHT... THAT THE PHANTOM NINJA IS A NINDROID?
NO, JAY WAS BEING FOOLISH.
GEE, THANKS.
YOU'RE WELCOME. NO, I HAVE SOME-THING ELSE IN MIND. IT'S JUST A THEORY, BUT IF I AM RIGHT...
THEN THE PHANTOM NINJA IS IN TERRIBLE DANGER.
WELL, WE CAN'T HELP GHOSTY IF WE CAN'T CATCH HIM.
I MAY HAVE AN IDEA THERE, TOO.
PLEASE, WHATEVER YOU DO, DO IT FAST. I AM WORRIED ABOUT SELIEL AND HER FATHER!
BELIEVE ME, SO AM I. WE WILL DO WHATEVER WE CAN.

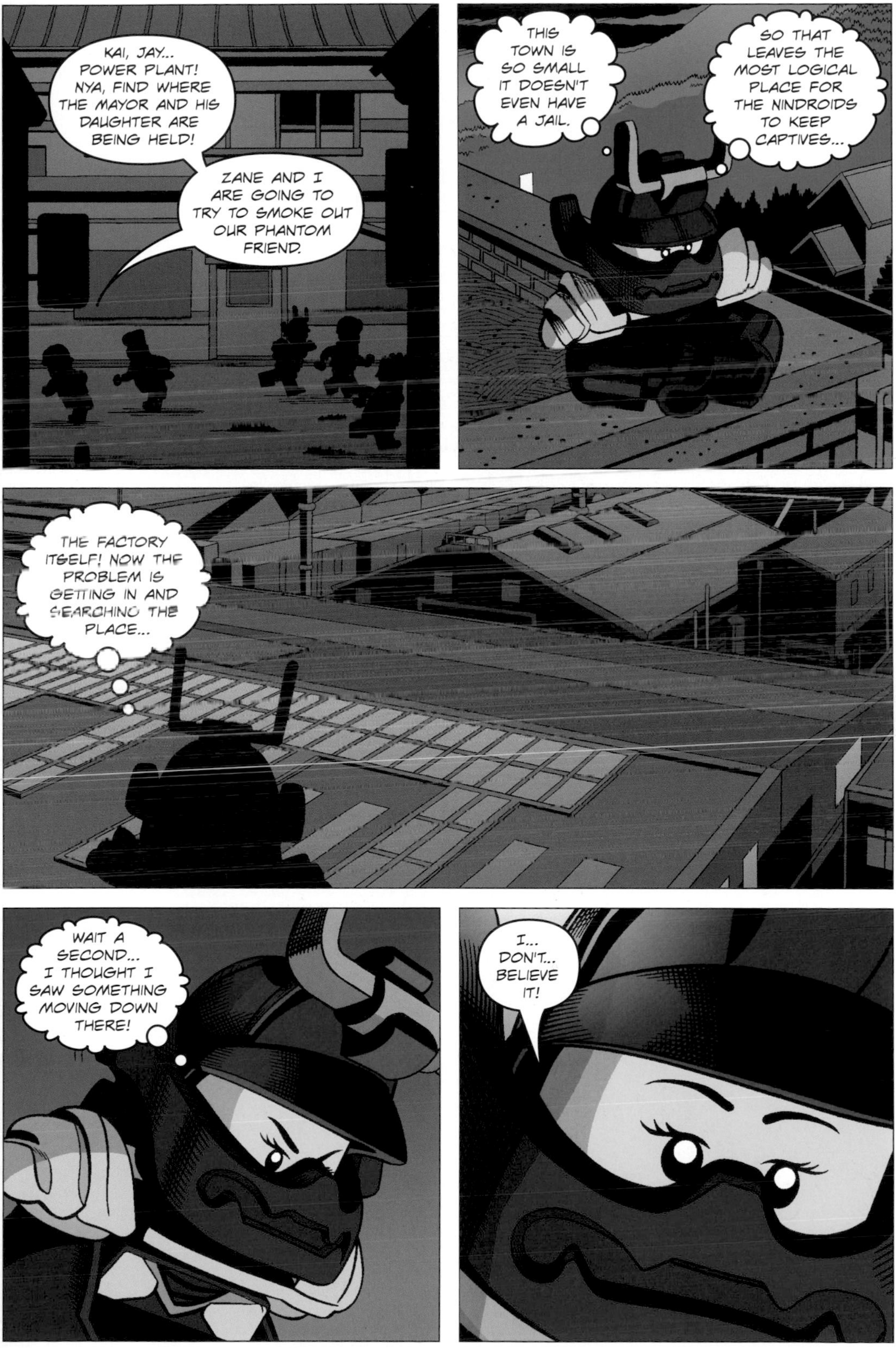
KAI, JAY... POWER PLANT! NYA, FIND WHERE THE MAYOR AND HIS DAUGHTER ARE BEING HELD!
ZANE AND I ARE GOING TO TRY TO SMOKE OUT OUR PHANTOM FRIEND.
THIS TOWN IS SO SMALL IT DOESN'T EVEN HAVE A JAIL.
SO THAT LEAVES THE MOST LOGICAL PLACE FOR THE NINDROIDS TO KEEP CAPTIVES...
THE FACTORY ITSELF! NOW THE PROBLEM IS GETTING IN AND SEARCHING THE PLACE...
WAIT A SECOND... I THOUGHT I SAW SOMETHING MOVING DOWN THERE!
I... DON'T... BELIEVE IT!

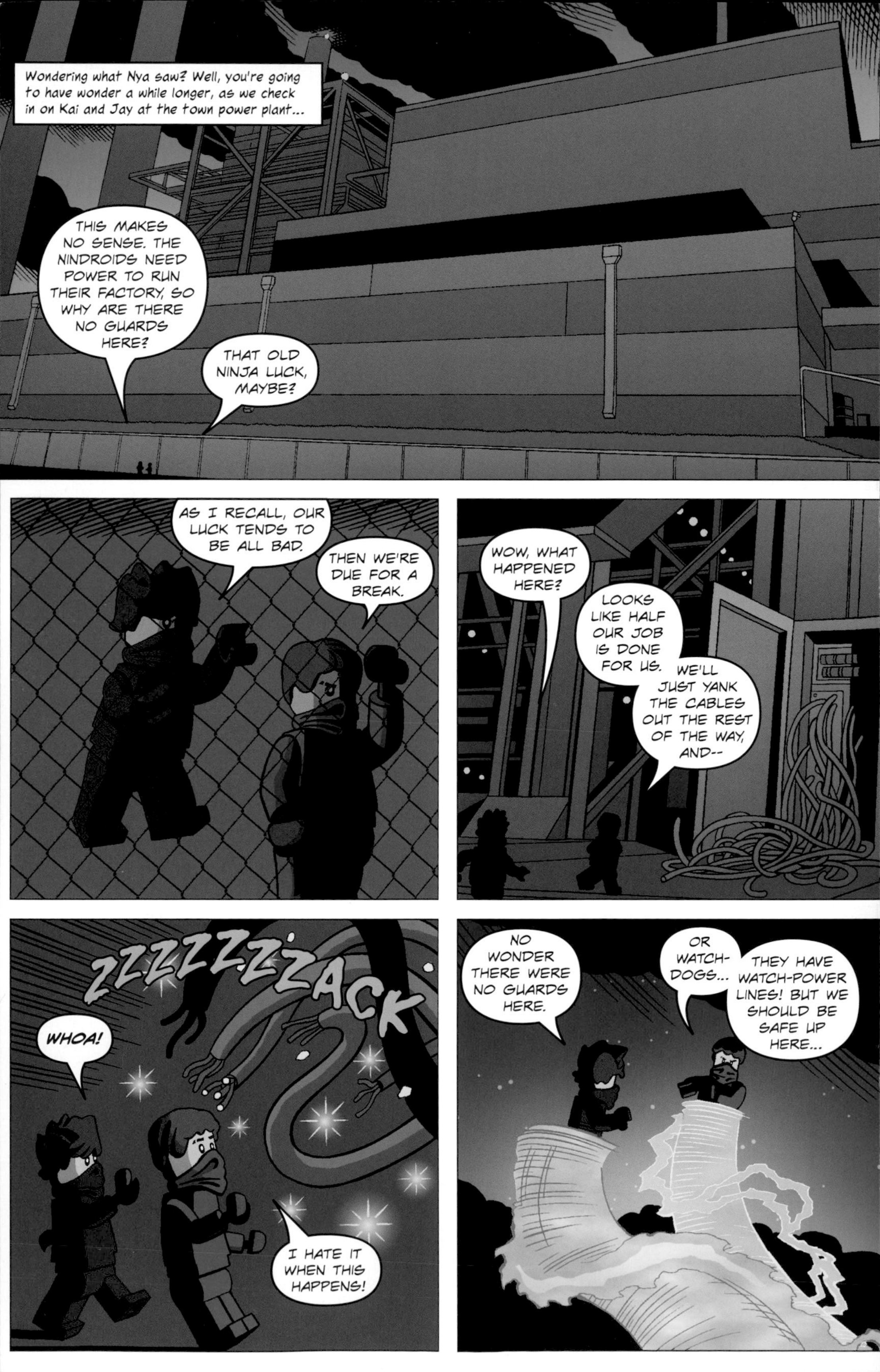
Wondering what Nya saw? Well, you're going to have wonder a while longer, as we check in on Kai and Jay at the town power plant...
THIS MAKES NO SENSE. THE NINDROIDS NEED POWER TO RUN THEIR FACTORY, SO WHY ARE THERE NO GUARDS HERE?
THAT OLD NINJA LUCK, MAYBE?
AS I RECALL, OUR LUCK TENDS TO BE ALL BAD.
THEN WE'RE DUE FOR A BREAK.
WOW, WHAT HAPPENED HERE?
LOOKS LIKE HALF OUR JOB IS DONE FOR US.
WE'LL JUST YANK THE CABLES OUT THE REST OF THE WAY, AND--
ZZZZZZZZACK
WHOA!
I HATE IT WHEN THIS HAPPENS!
NO WONDER THERE WERE NO GUARDS HERE.
OR WATCH-DOGS...
THEY HAVE WATCH-POWER LINES! BUT WE SHOULD BE SAFE UP HERE...

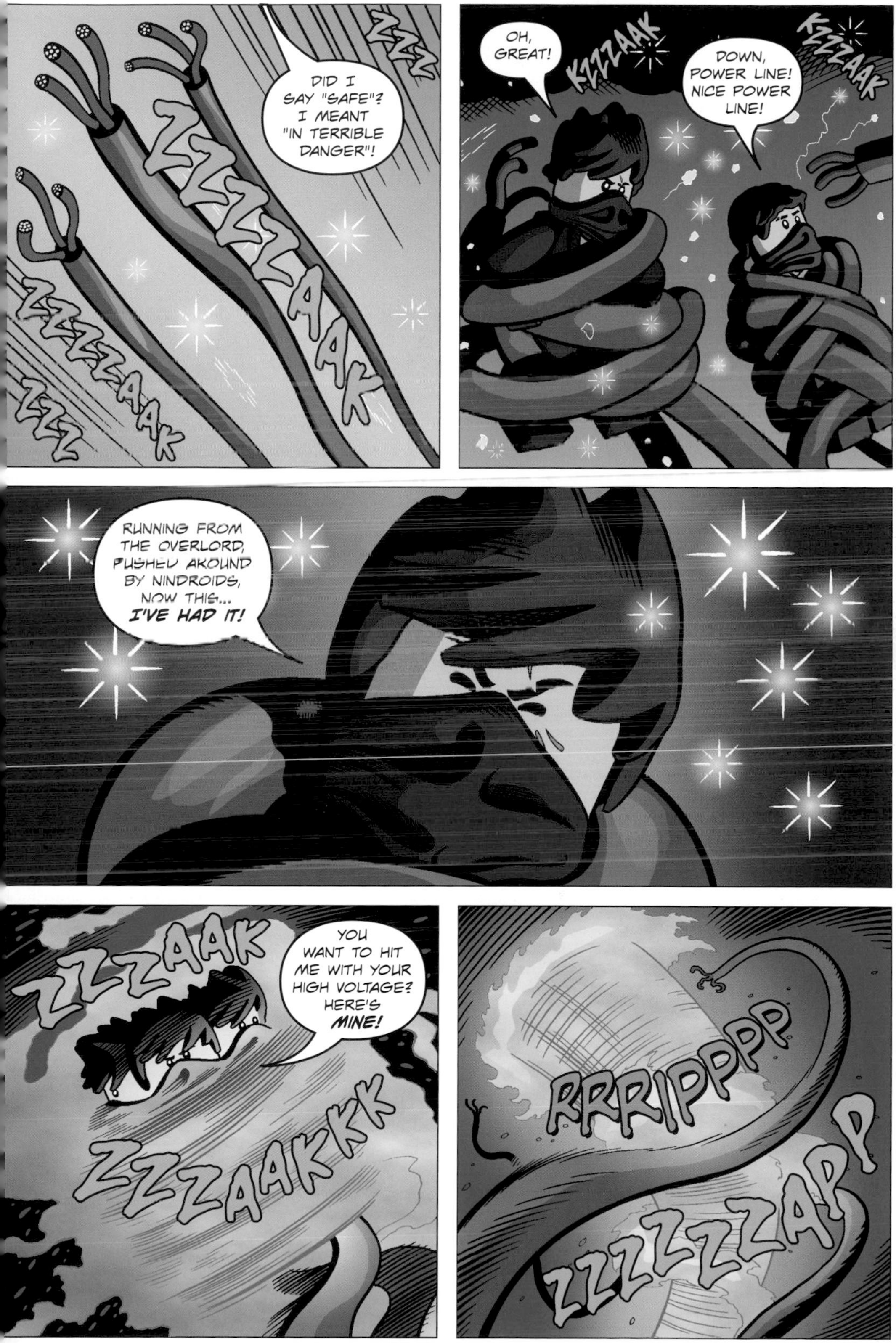
ZZZ
DID I SAY "SAFE"? I MEANT "IN TERRIBLE DANGER"!
ZZZZZZAAAK
ZZZZZAAAK
ZZZ
OH, GREAT!
KZZZAAK
DOWN, POWER LINE! NICE POWER LINE!
KZZZAAK
RUNNING FROM THE OVERLORD, PUSHED AROUND BY NINDROIDS, NOW THIS... I'VE HAD IT!
ZZZZAAK
YOU WANT TO HIT ME WITH YOUR HIGH VOLTAGE? HERE'S MINE!
ZZZZAAKKK
RRRIPPPP
ZZZZZZZAPP

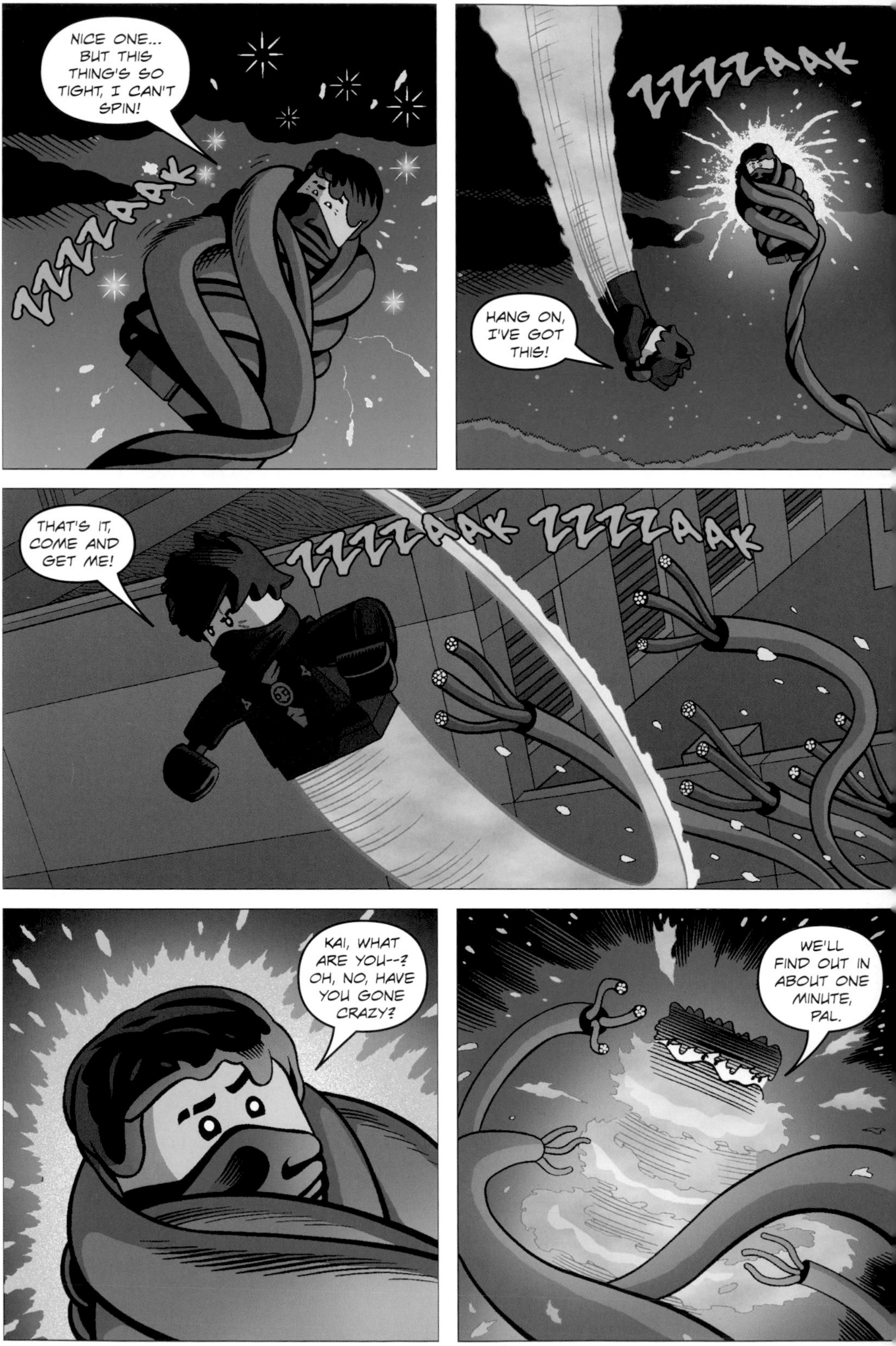
NICE ONE... BUT THIS THING'S SO TIGHT, I CAN'T SPIN!
ZZZZAAK
ZZZZAAK
HANG ON, I'VE GOT THIS!
THAT'S IT, COME AND GET ME!
ZZZZZAAK ZZZZZAAK
KAI, WHAT ARE YOU--? OH, NO, HAVE YOU GONE CRAZY?
WE'LL FIND OUT IN ABOUT ONE MINUTE, PAL.

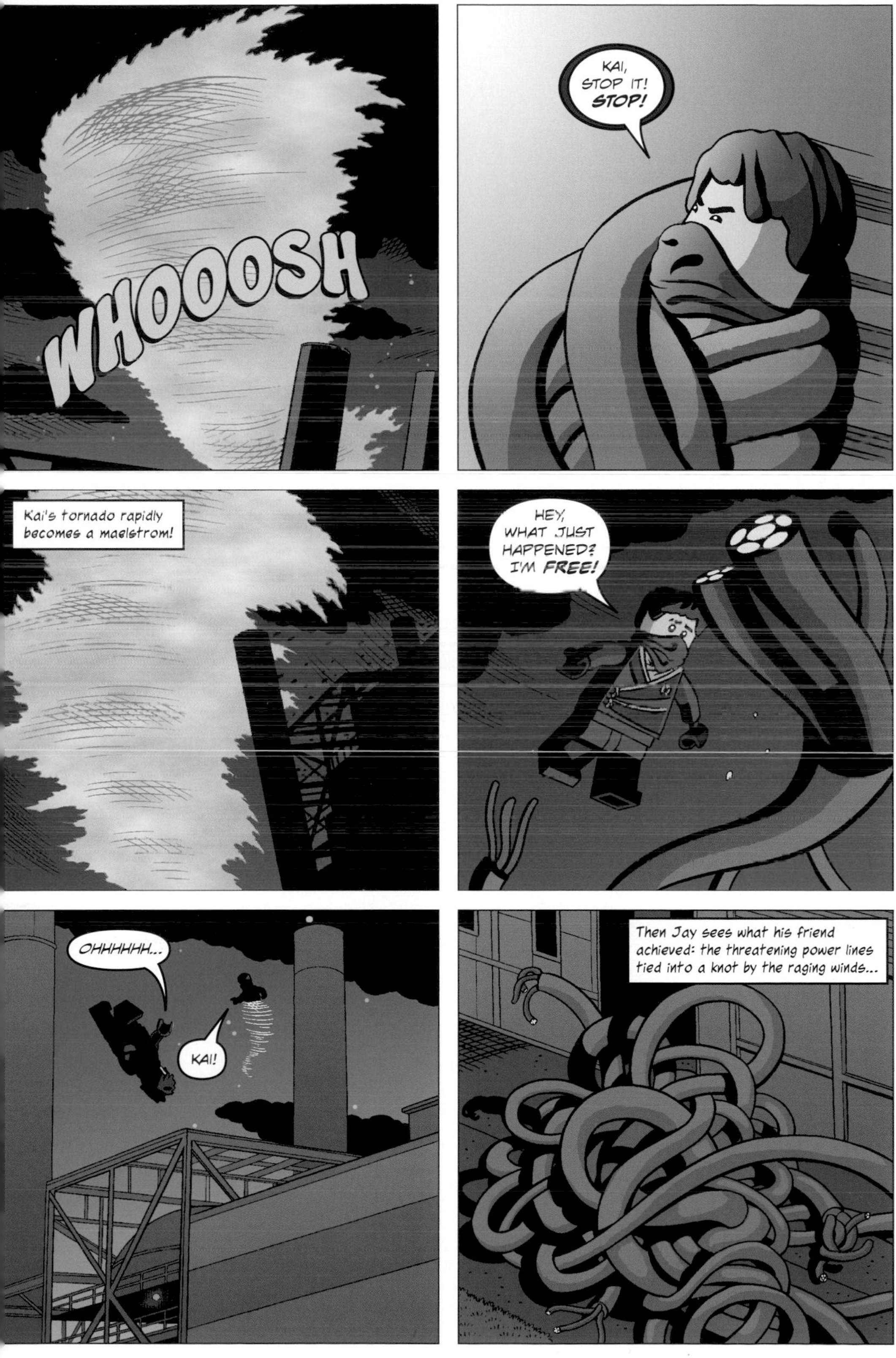
WHOOOSH
KAI, STOP IT! STOP!
Kai's tornado rapidly becomes a maelstrom!
HEY, WHAT JUST HAPPENED? I'M FREE!
OHHHHHH...
KAI!
Then Jay sees what his friend achieved: the threatening power lines tied into a knot by the raging winds...

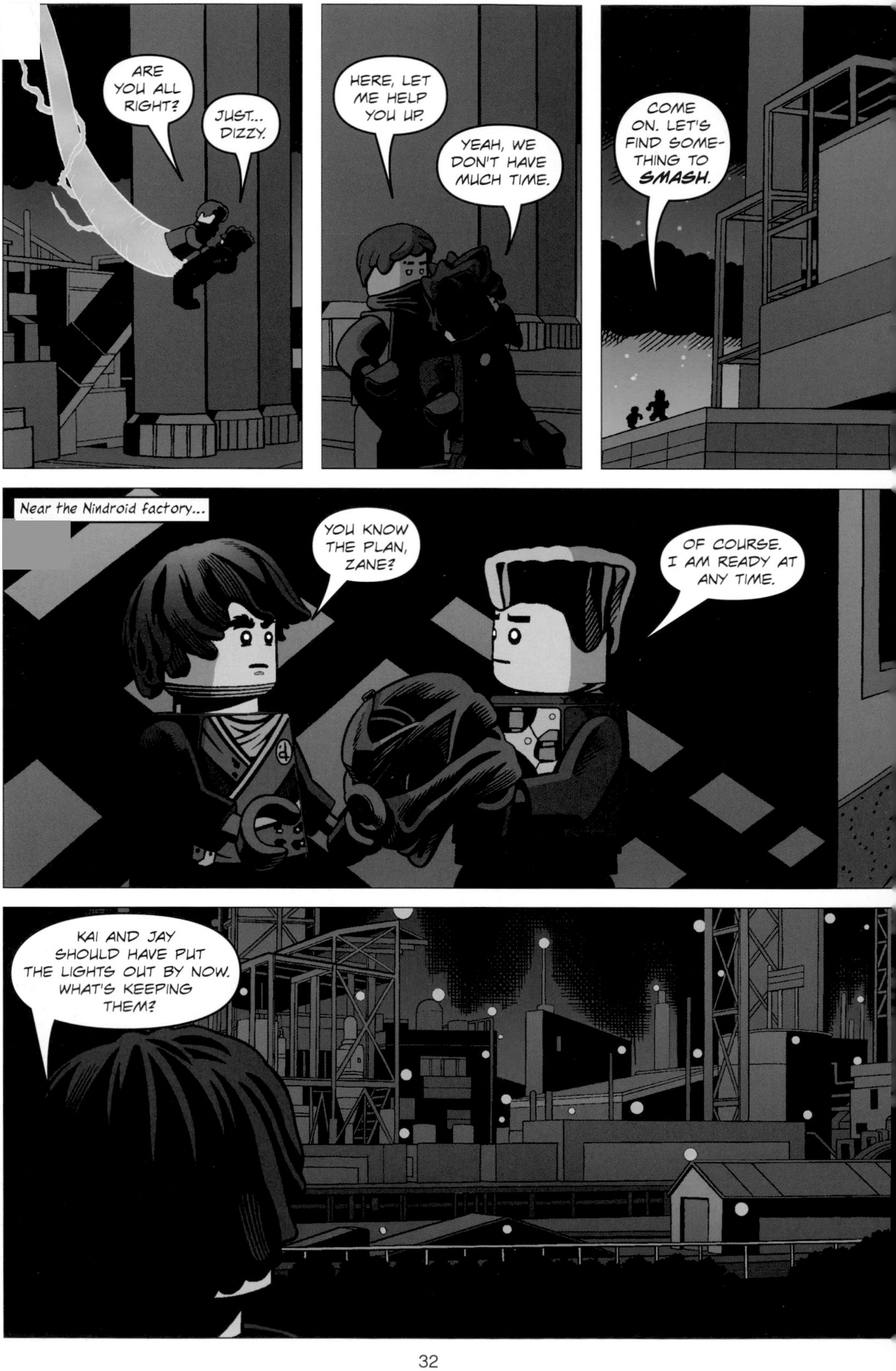
ARE YOU ALL RIGHT?
JUST... DIZZY.
HERE, LET ME HELP YOU UP.
YEAH, WE DON'T HAVE MUCH TIME.
COME ON. LET'S FIND SOME-THING TO SMASH.
Near the Nindroid factory...
YOU KNOW THE PLAN, ZANE?
OF COURSE. I AM READY AT ANY TIME.
KAI AND JAY SHOULD HAVE PUT THE LIGHTS OUT BY NOW. WHAT'S KEEPING THEM?

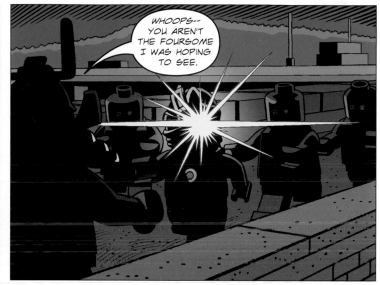

And on a nearby rooftop...

WOW, WAIT UNTIL I TELL THE GUYS ABOUT *THIS!*

WHOOPS-- YOU AREN'T THE FOURSOME I WAS HOPING TO SEE.

WELL, YOU'RE NOT GOING TO CAPTURE ME THAT EASILY!

OR --:OOF!:-- MAYBE YOU ARE.

ANALYSIS: HUMAN FEMALE. PREVIOUS ENCOUNTER: UNSATISFACTORY.

THREAT LEVEL: HIGHLY DANGEROUS.

RECOMMENDATION: IMMEDIATE DESTRUCTION.

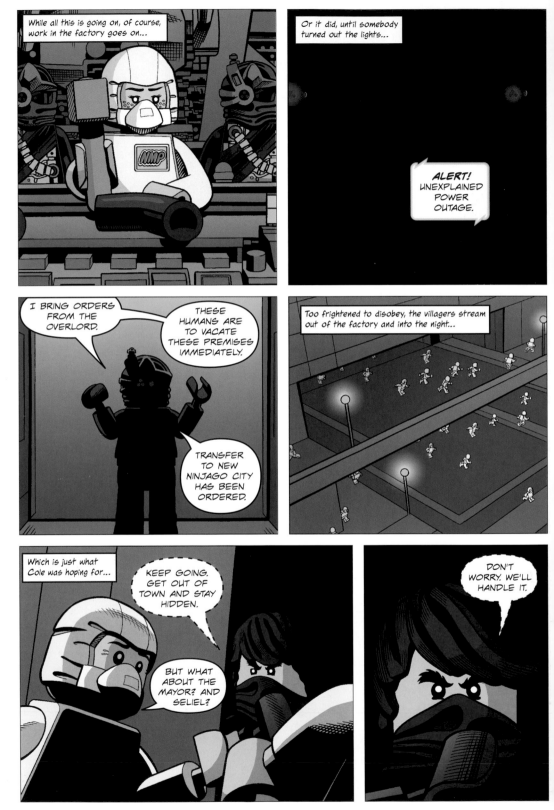

While all this is going on, of course, work in the factory goes on...

Or it did, until somebody turned out the lights...

ALERT! UNEXPLAINED POWER OUTAGE.

I BRING ORDERS FROM THE OVERLORD.

THESE HUMANS ARE TO VACATE THESE PREMISES IMMEDIATELY.

TRANSFER TO NEW NINJAGO CITY HAS BEEN ORDERED.

Too frightened to disobey, the villagers stream out of the factory and into the night...

Which is just what Cole was hoping for...

KEEP GOING. GET OUT OF TOWN AND STAY HIDDEN.

BUT WHAT ABOUT THE MAYOR? AND SELIEL?

DON'T WORRY. WE'LL HANDLE IT.

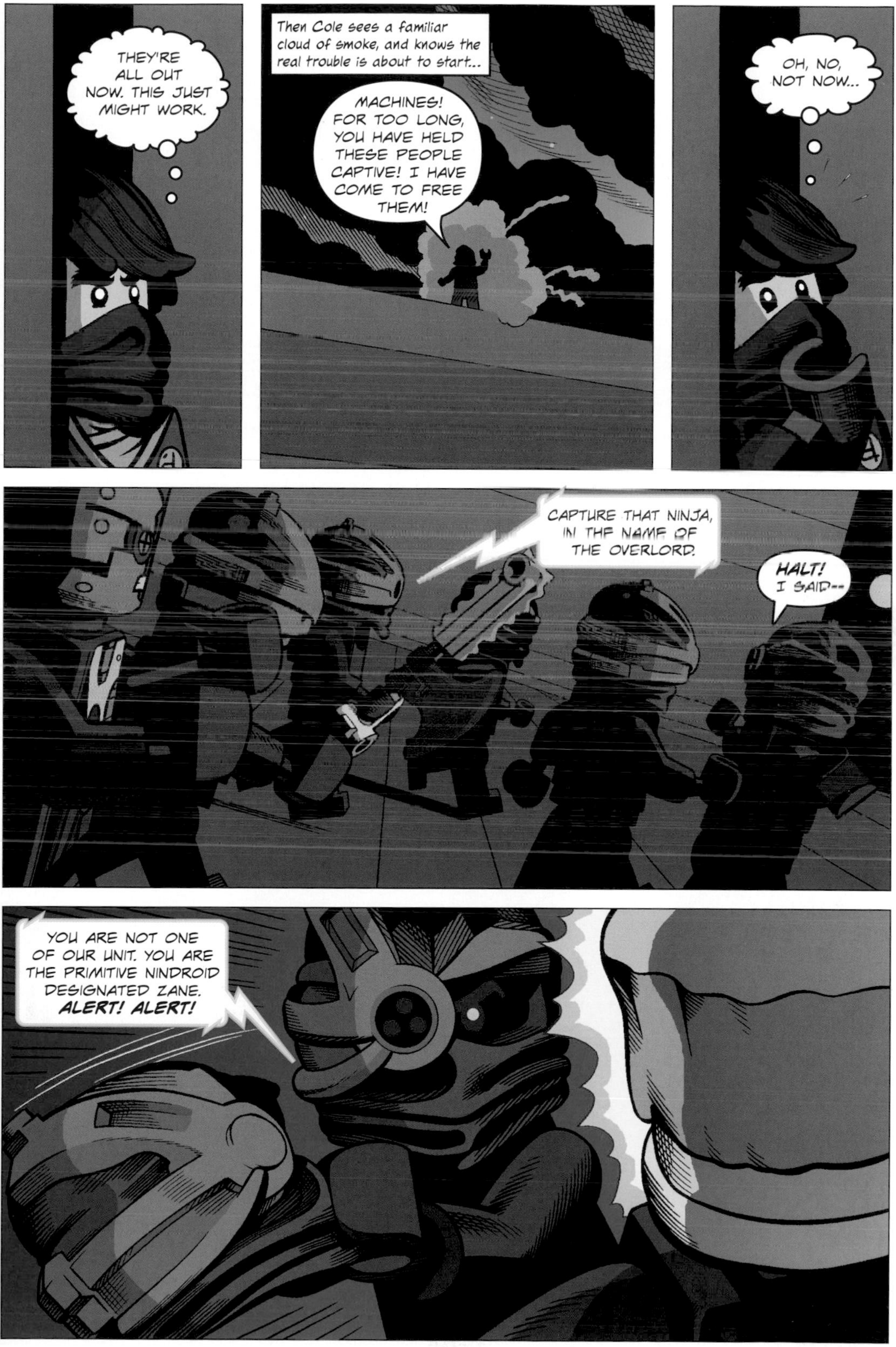
THEY'RE ALL OUT NOW. THIS JUST MIGHT WORK.
Then Cole sees a familiar cloud of smoke, and knows the real trouble is about to start...
MACHINES! FOR TOO LONG, YOU HAVE HELD THESE PEOPLE CAPTIVE! I HAVE COME TO FREE THEM!
OH, NO, NOT NOW...
CAPTURE THAT NINJA, IN THE NAME OF THE OVERLORD.
HALT! I SAID--
YOU ARE NOT ONE OF OUR UNIT. YOU ARE THE PRIMITIVE NINDROID DESIGNATED ZANE. ALERT! ALERT!

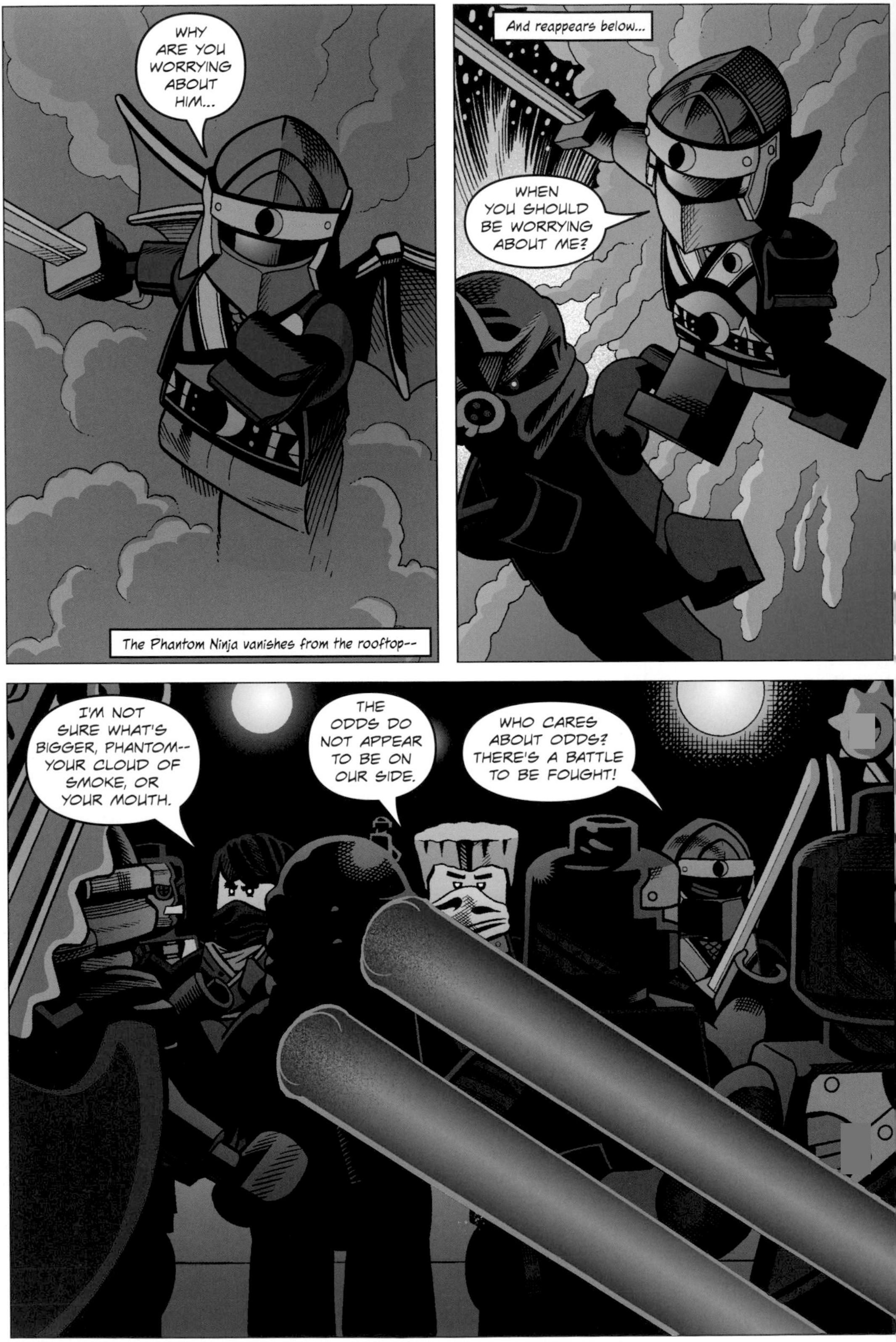
WHY ARE YOU WORRYING ABOUT HIM...
The Phantom Ninja vanishes from the rooftop--
And reappears below...
WHEN YOU SHOULD BE WORRYING ABOUT ME?
I'M NOT SURE WHAT'S BIGGER, PHANTOM-- YOUR CLOUD OF SMOKE, OR YOUR MOUTH.
THE ODDS DO NOT APPEAR TO BE ON OUR SIDE.
WHO CARES ABOUT ODDS? THERE'S A BATTLE TO BE FOUGHT!

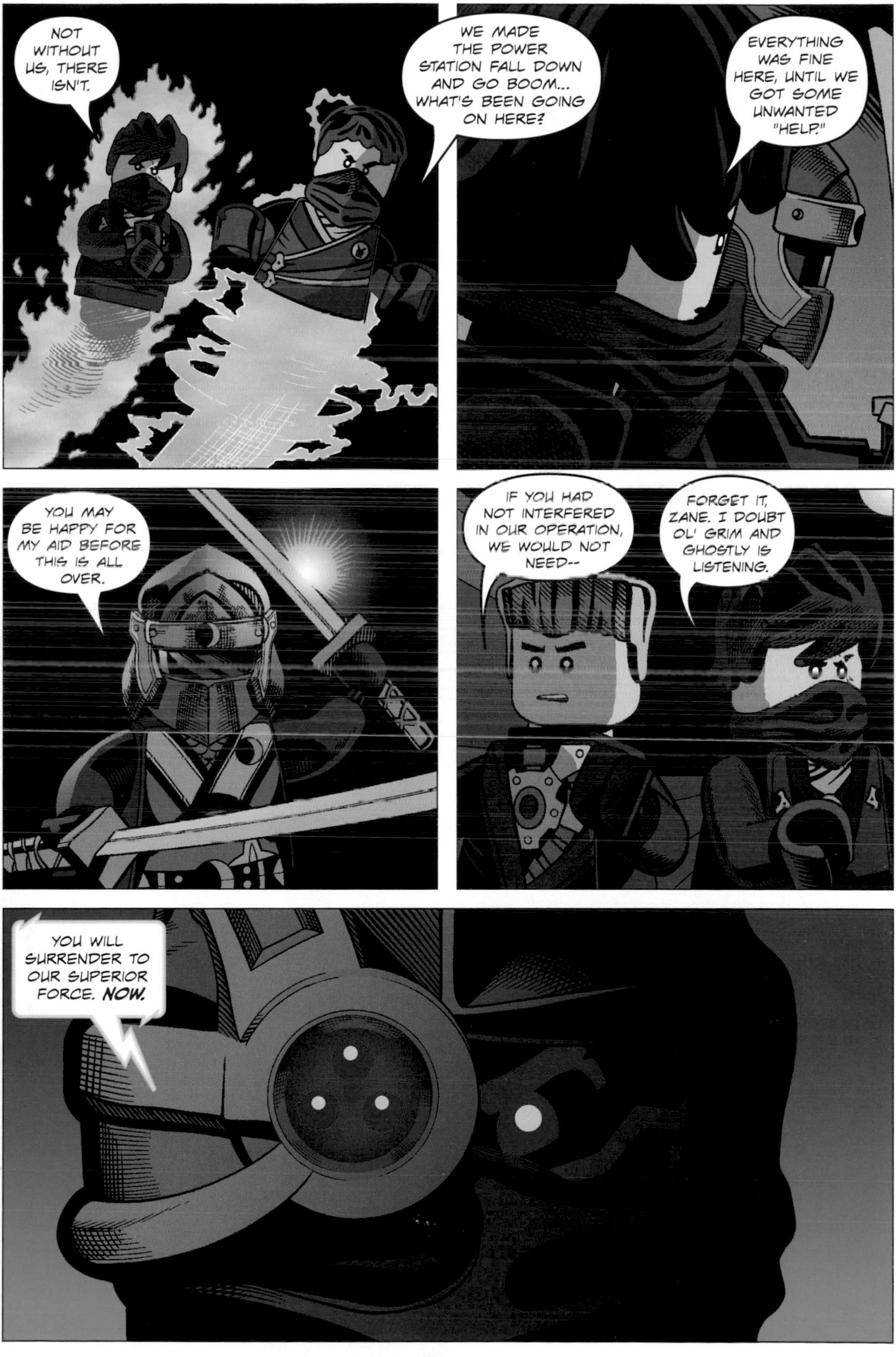
NOT WITHOUT US, THERE ISN'T.
WE MADE THE POWER STATION FALL DOWN AND GO BOOM... WHAT'S BEEN GOING ON HERE?
EVERYTHING WAS FINE HERE, UNTIL WE GOT SOME UNWANTED "HELP."
YOU MAY BE HAPPY FOR MY AID BEFORE THIS IS ALL OVER.
IF YOU HAD NOT INTERFERED IN OUR OPERATION, WE WOULD NOT NEED--
FORGET IT, ZANE. I DOUBT OL' GRIM AND GHOSTLY IS LISTENING.
YOU WILL SURRENDER TO OUR SUPERIOR FORCE. NOW.

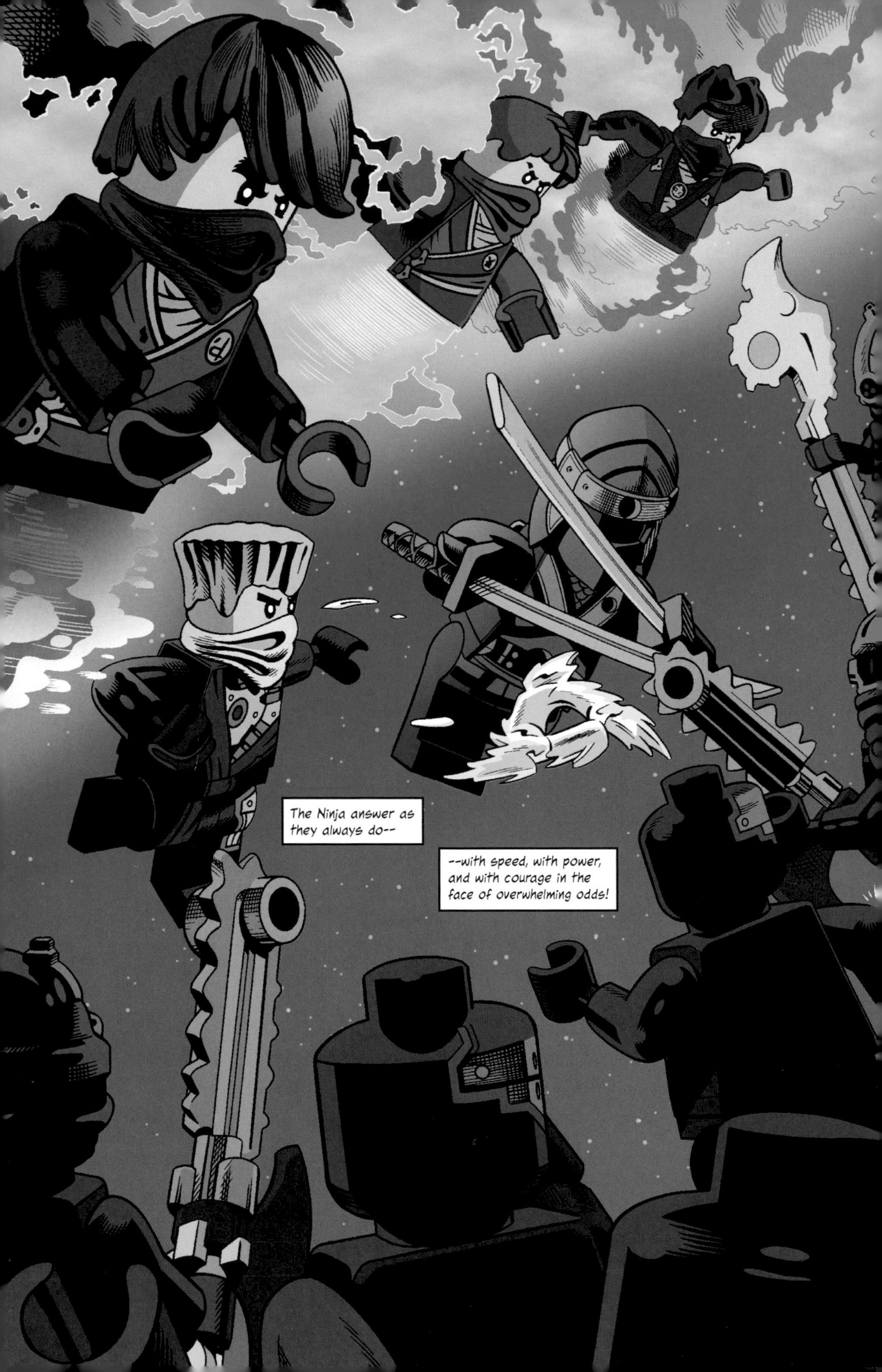
The Ninja answer as they always do--
--with speed, with power, and with courage in the face of overwhelming odds!

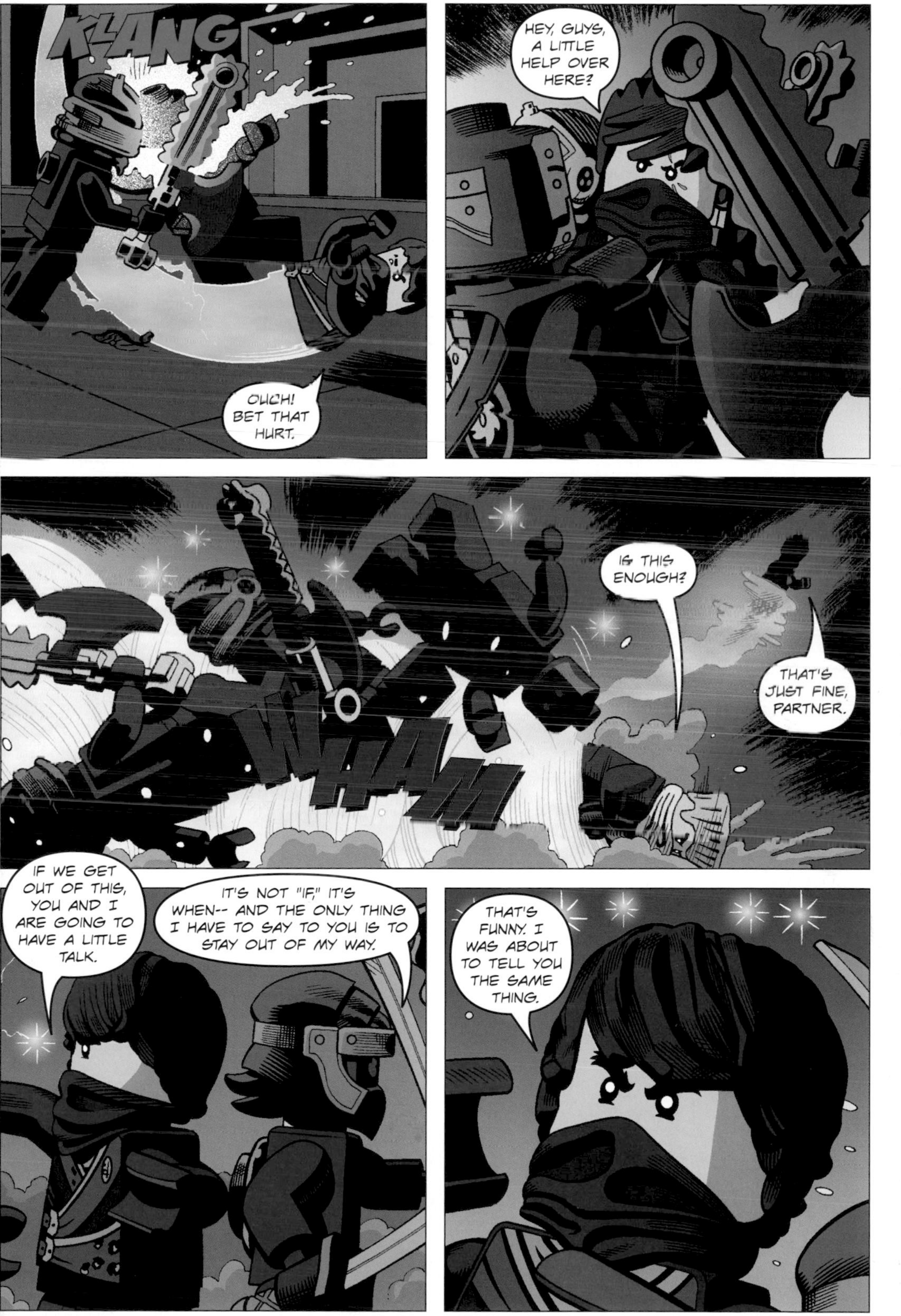
KLANG
OUCH! BET THAT HURT.
HEY, GUYS, A LITTLE HELP OVER HERE?
IS THIS ENOUGH?
WHAM
THAT'S JUST FINE, PARTNER.
IF WE GET OUT OF THIS, YOU AND I ARE GOING TO HAVE A LITTLE TALK.
IT'S NOT "IF," IT'S WHEN-- AND THE ONLY THING I HAVE TO SAY TO YOU IS TO STAY OUT OF MY WAY.
THAT'S FUNNY. I WAS ABOUT TO TELL YOU THE SAME THING.

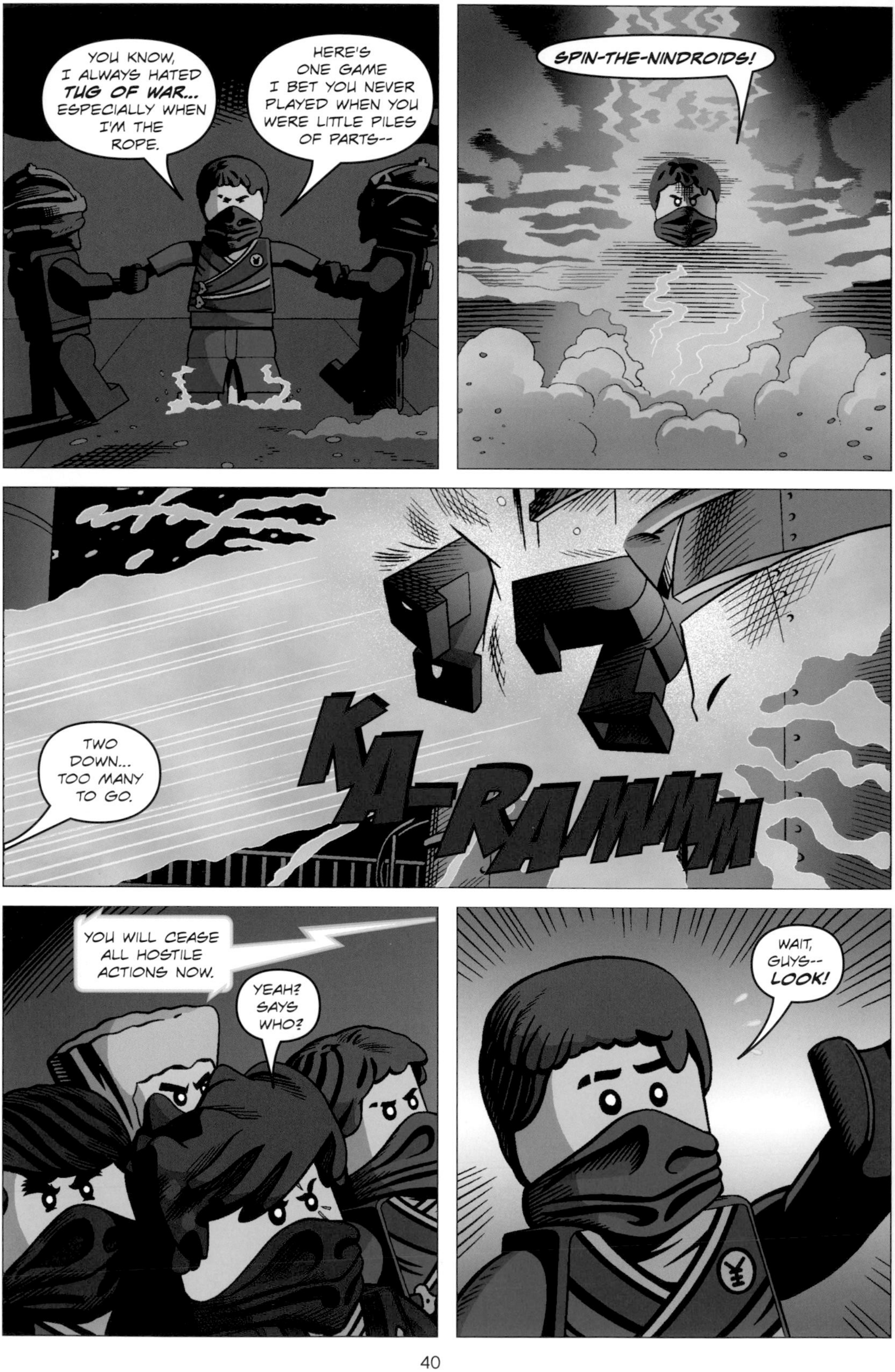

YOU KNOW, I ALWAYS HATED TUG OF WAR... ESPECIALLY WHEN I'M THE ROPE.
HERE'S ONE GAME I BET YOU NEVER PLAYED WHEN YOU WERE LITTLE PILES OF PARTS--
SPIN-THE-NINDROIDS!
KA-RAMMM
TWO DOWN... TOO MANY TO GO.
YOU WILL CEASE ALL HOSTILE ACTIONS NOW.
YEAH? SAYS WHO?
WAIT, GUYS-- LOOK!

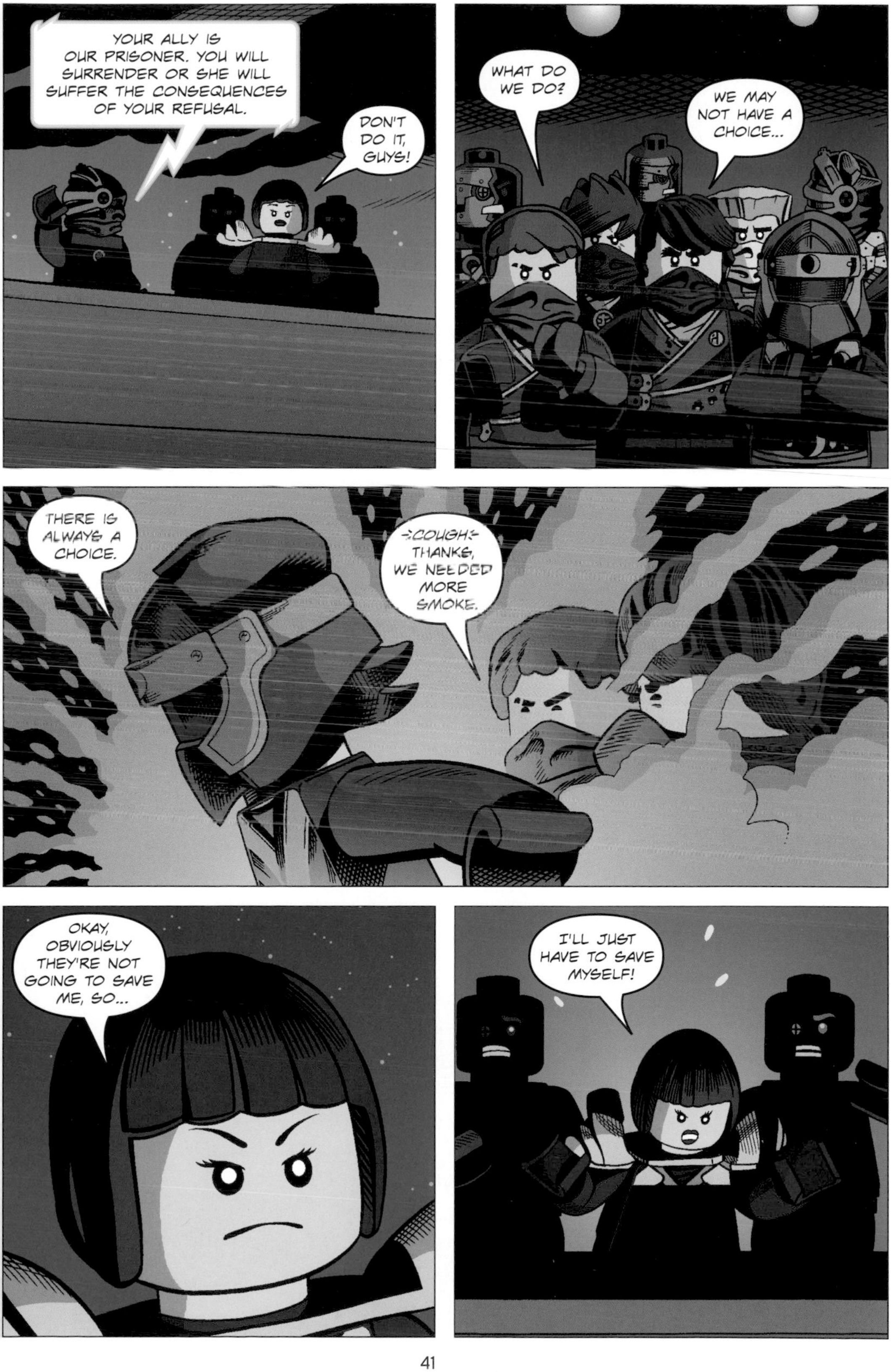
YOUR ALLY IS OUR PRISONER. YOU WILL SURRENDER OR SHE WILL SUFFER THE CONSEQUENCES OF YOUR REFUSAL.
DON'T DO IT, GUYS!
WHAT DO WE DO?
WE MAY NOT HAVE A CHOICE...
THERE IS ALWAYS A CHOICE.
COUGH THANKS, WE NEEDED MORE SMOKE.
OKAY, OBVIOUSLY THEY'RE NOT GOING TO SAVE ME, SO...
I'LL JUST HAVE TO SAVE MYSELF!

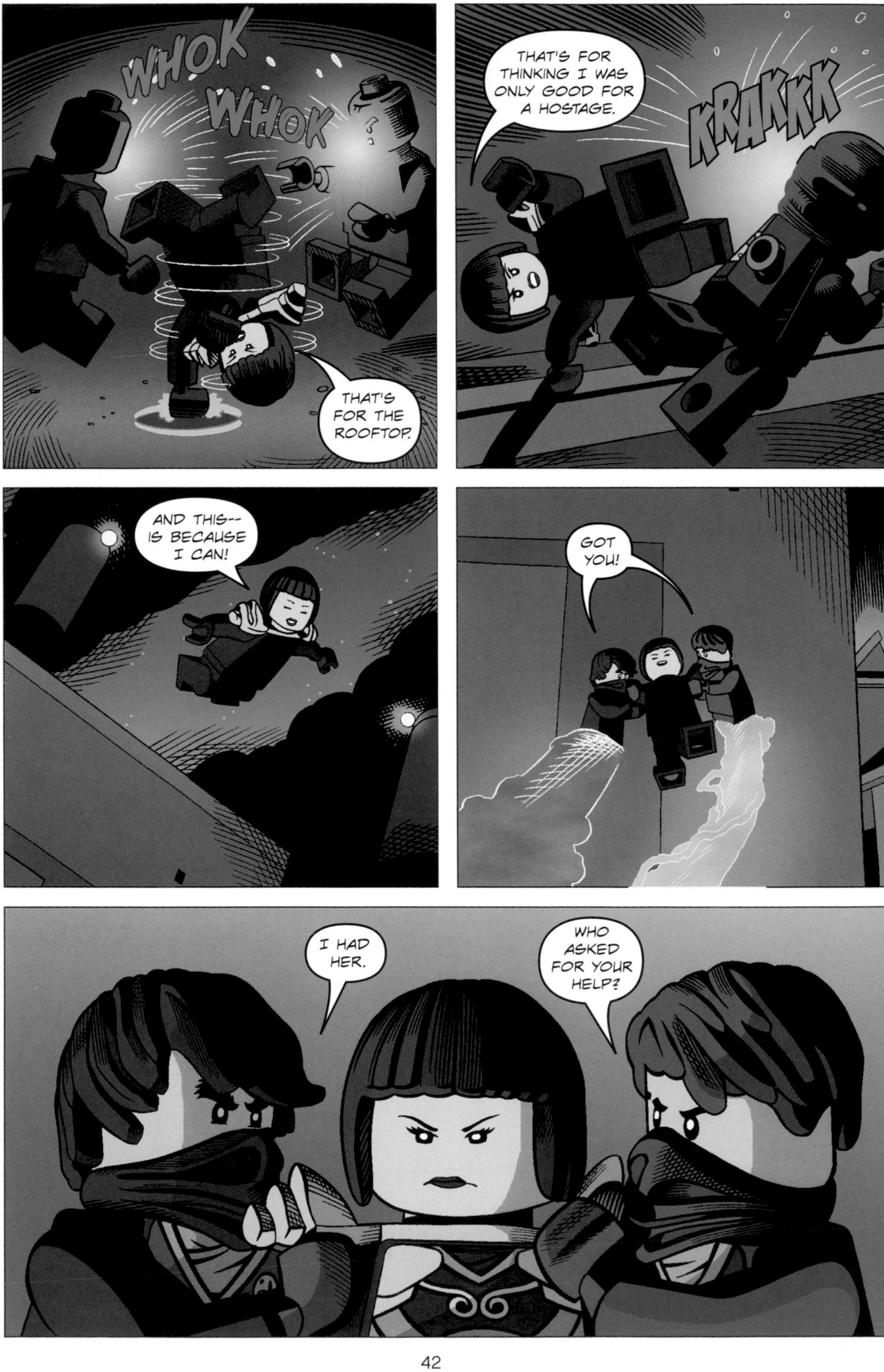
WHOK
WHOK
THAT'S FOR THE ROOFTOP.
THAT'S FOR THINKING I WAS ONLY GOOD FOR A HOSTAGE.
KRAKKK
AND THIS-- IS BECAUSE I CAN!
GOT YOU!
I HAD HER.
WHO ASKED FOR YOUR HELP?

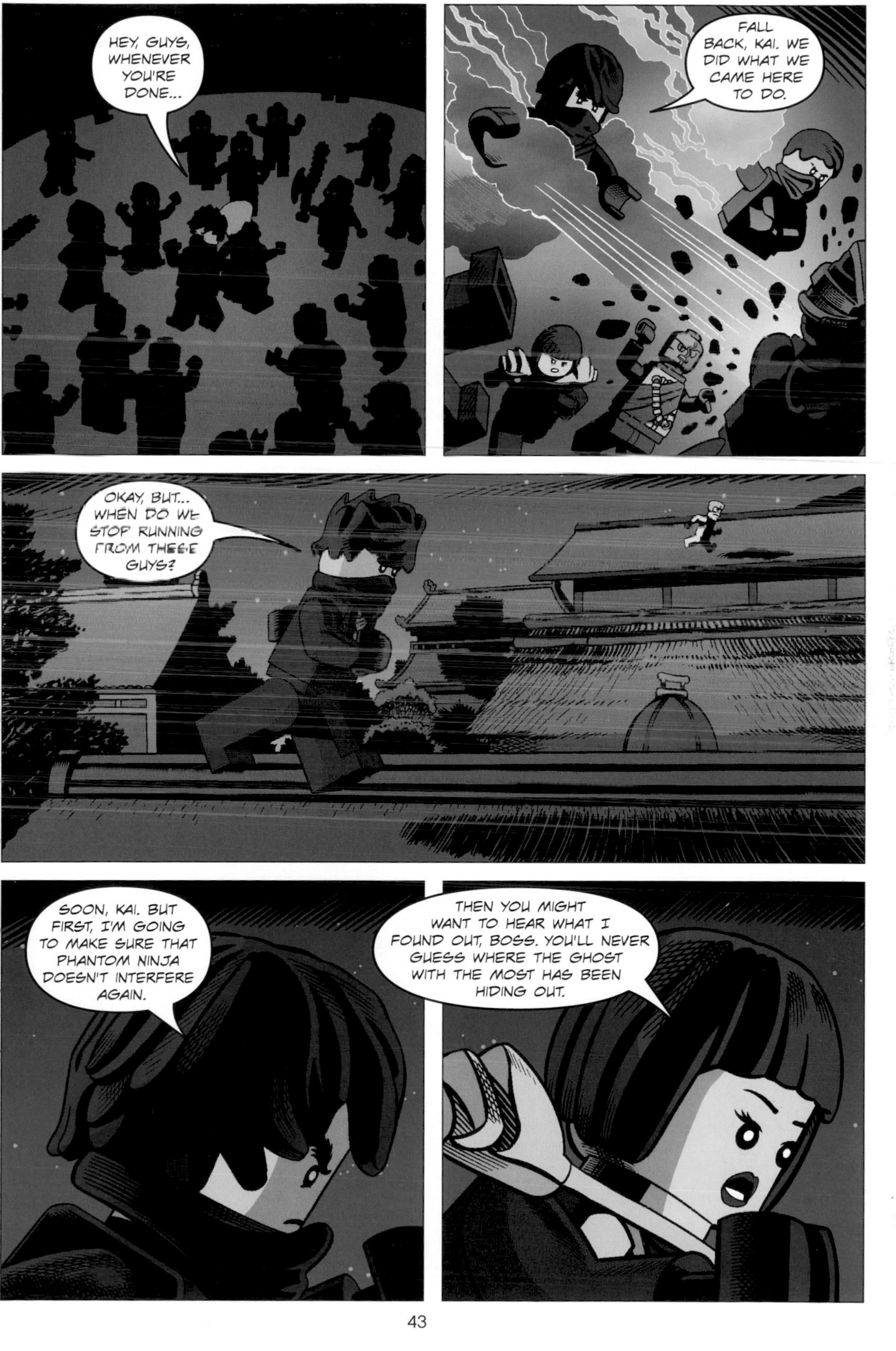
HEY, GUYS, WHENEVER YOU'RE DONE...
FALL BACK, KAI. WE DID WHAT WE CAME HERE TO DO.
OKAY, BUT... WHEN DO WE STOP RUNNING FROM THESE GUYS?
SOON, KAI. BUT FIRST, I'M GOING TO MAKE SURE THAT PHANTOM NINJA DOESN'T INTERFERE AGAIN.
THEN YOU MIGHT WANT TO HEAR WHAT I FOUND OUT, BOSS. YOU'LL NEVER GUESS WHERE THE GHOST WITH THE MOST HAS BEEN HIDING OUT.

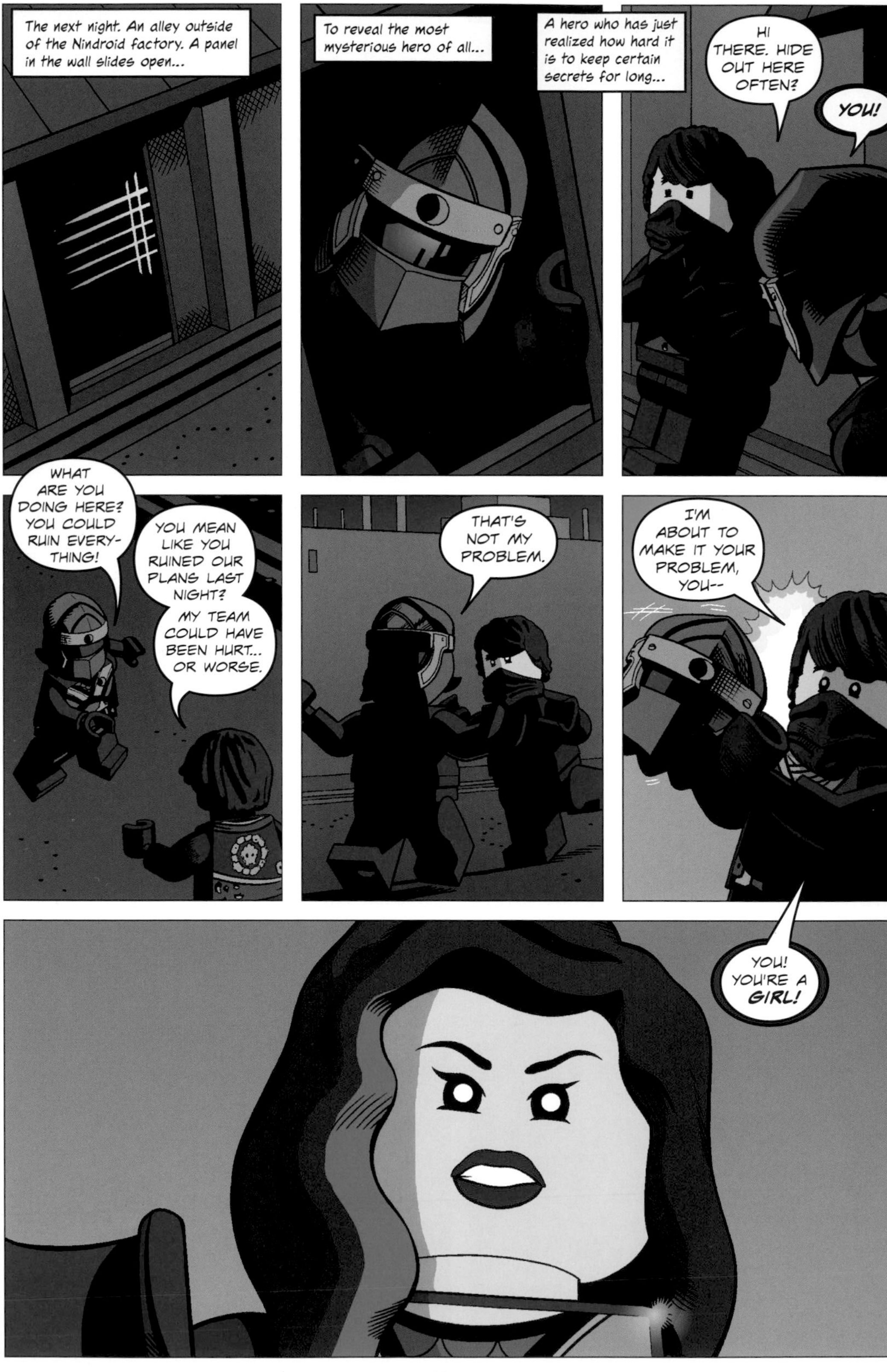
The next night. An alley outside of the Nindroid factory. A panel in the wall slides open...
To reveal the most mysterious hero of all...
A hero who has just realized how hard it is to keep certain secrets for long...
HI THERE. HIDE OUT HERE OFTEN?
YOU!
WHAT ARE YOU DOING HERE? YOU COULD RUIN EVERY-THING!
YOU MEAN LIKE YOU RUINED OUR PLANS LAST NIGHT?
MY TEAM COULD HAVE BEEN HURT... OR WORSE.
THAT'S NOT MY PROBLEM.
I'M ABOUT TO MAKE IT YOUR PROBLEM, YOU--
YOU! YOU'RE A GIRL!

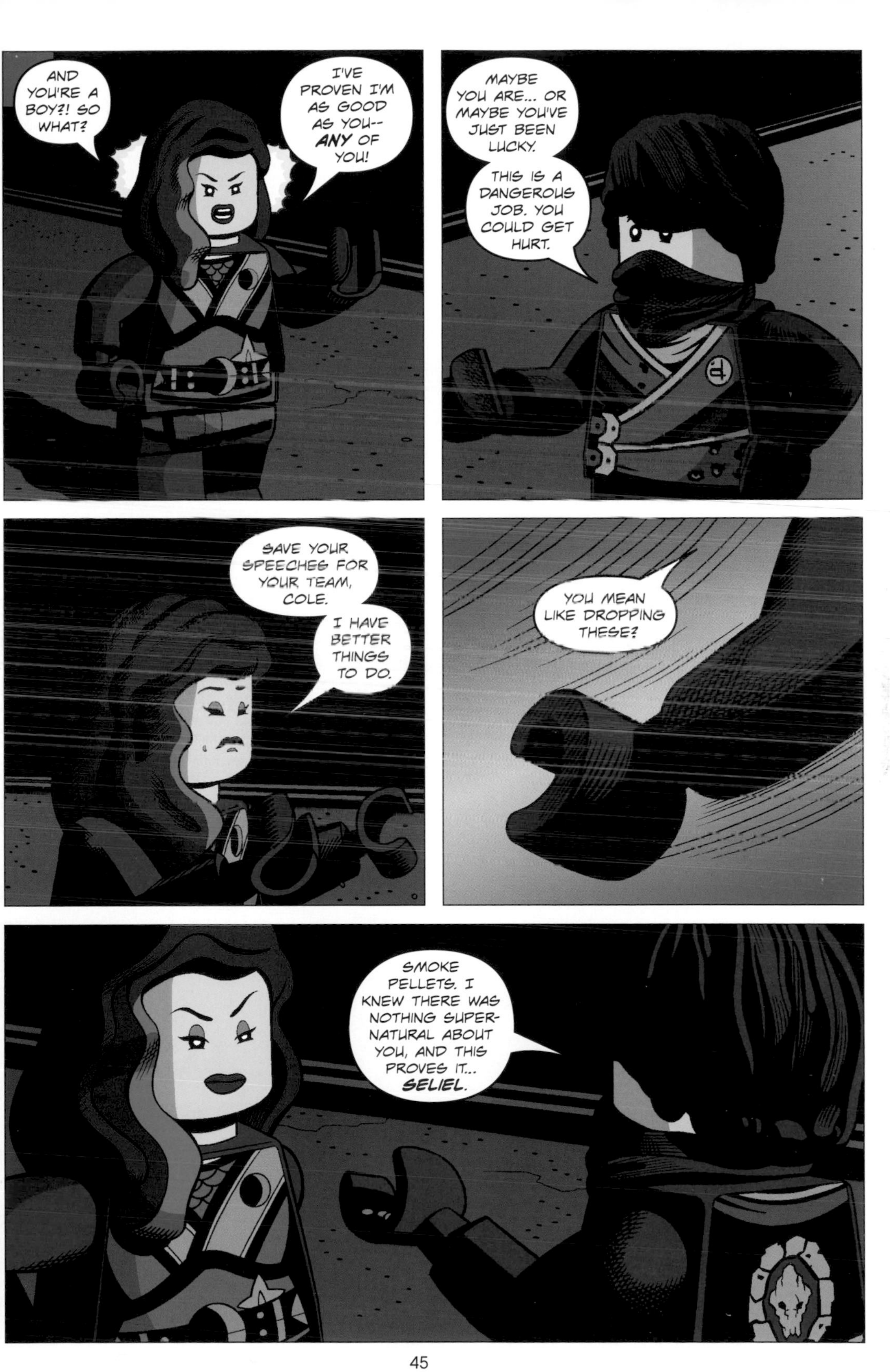
AND YOU'RE A BOY?! SO WHAT?
I'VE PROVEN I'M AS GOOD AS YOU-- ANY OF YOU!
MAYBE YOU ARE... OR MAYBE YOU'VE JUST BEEN LUCKY.
THIS IS A DANGEROUS JOB. YOU COULD GET HURT.
SAVE YOUR SPEECHES FOR YOUR TEAM, COLE.
I HAVE BETTER THINGS TO DO.
YOU MEAN LIKE DROPPING THESE?
SMOKE PELLETS. I KNEW THERE WAS NOTHING SUPER-NATURAL ABOUT YOU, AND THIS PROVES IT... SELIEL.

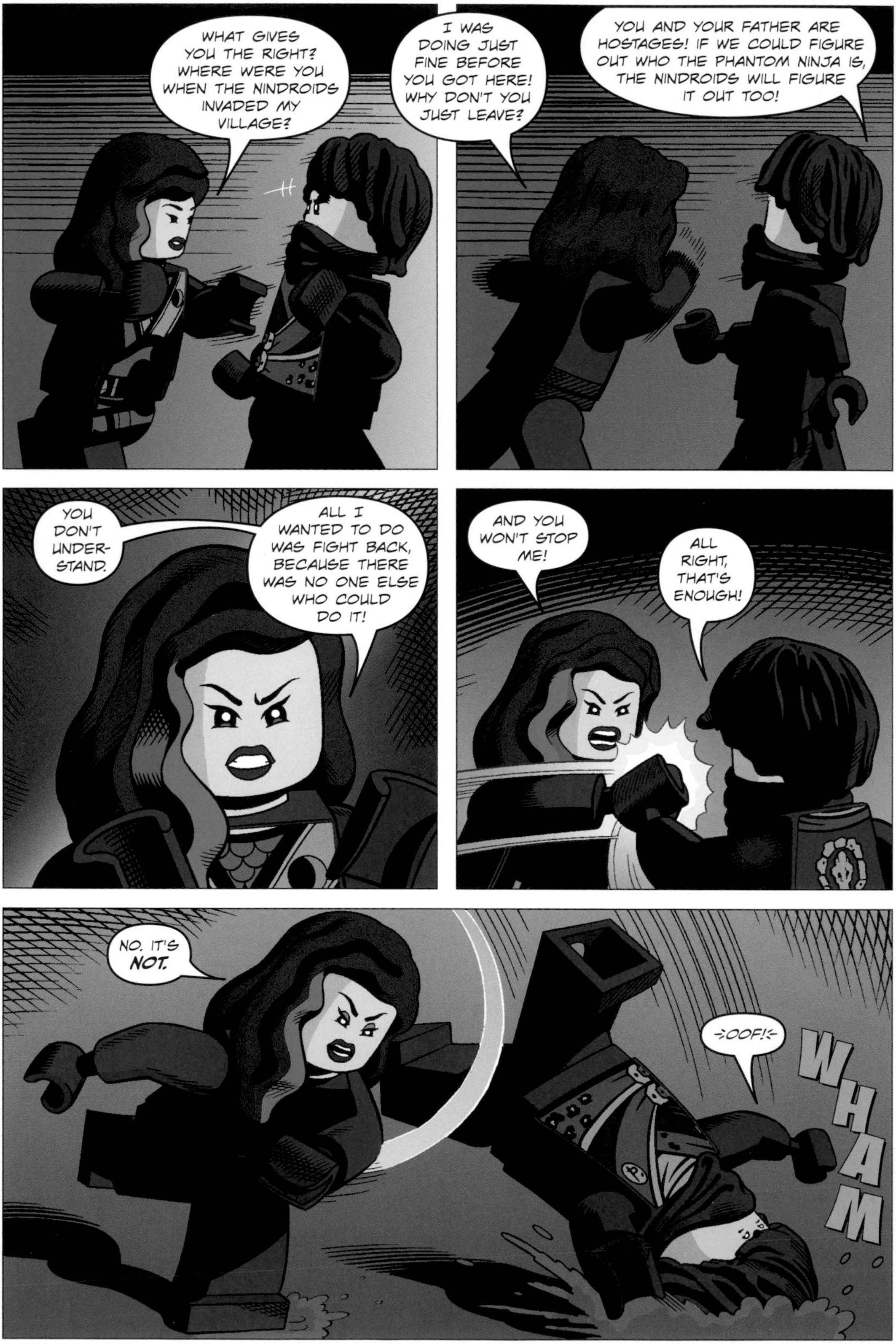
WHAT GIVES YOU THE RIGHT? WHERE WERE YOU WHEN THE NINDROIDS INVADED MY VILLAGE?
I WAS DOING JUST FINE BEFORE YOU GOT HERE! WHY DON'T YOU JUST LEAVE?
YOU AND YOUR FATHER ARE HOSTAGES! IF WE COULD FIGURE OUT WHO THE PHANTOM NINJA IS, THE NINDROIDS WILL FIGURE IT OUT TOO!
YOU DON'T UNDER-STAND.
ALL I WANTED TO DO WAS FIGHT BACK, BECAUSE THERE WAS NO ONE ELSE WHO COULD DO IT!
AND YOU WON'T STOP ME!
ALL RIGHT, THAT'S ENOUGH!
NO. IT'S **NOT.**
OOF!
WHAM

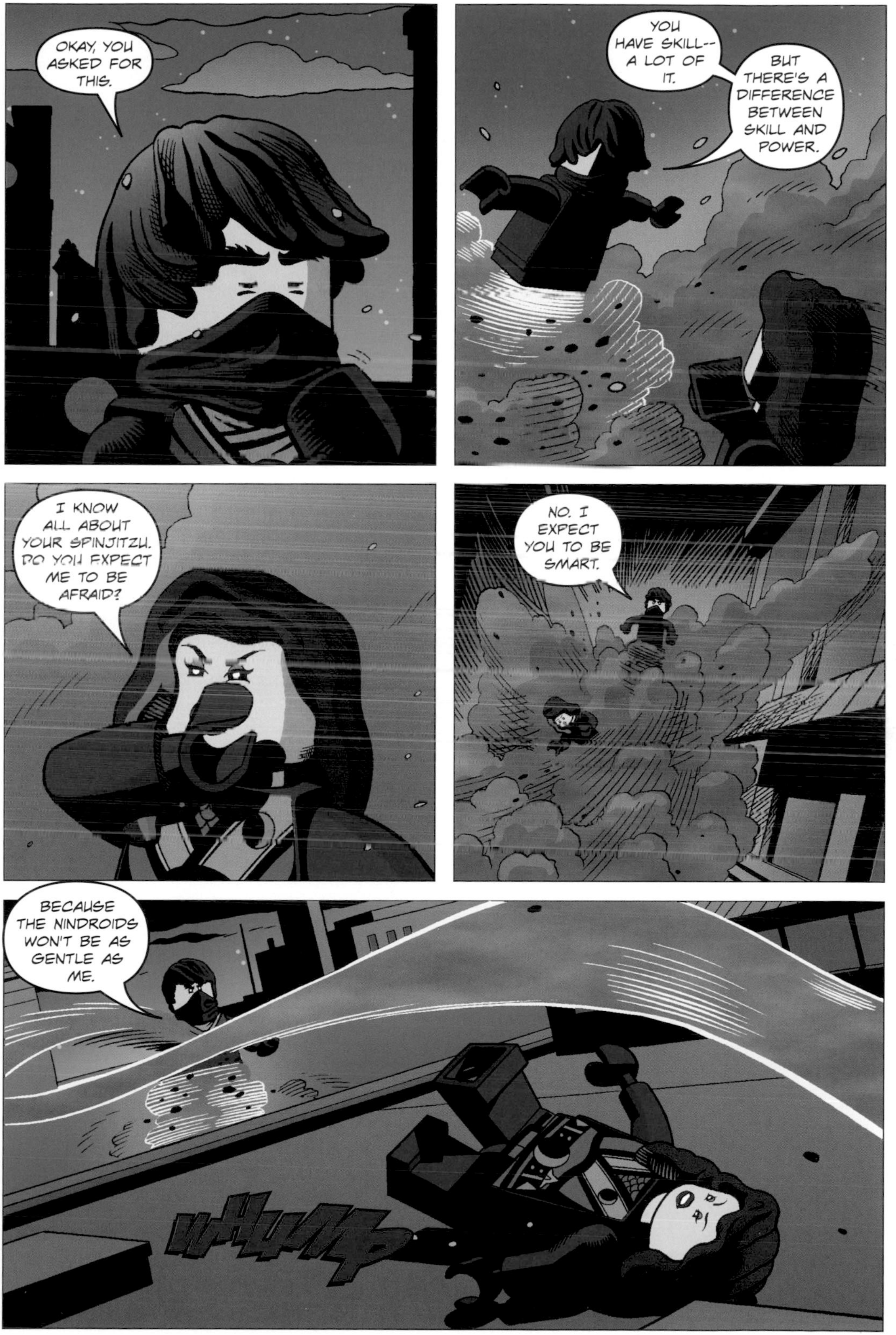
OKAY, YOU ASKED FOR THIS.
YOU HAVE SKILL-- A LOT OF IT.
BUT THERE'S A DIFFERENCE BETWEEN SKILL AND POWER.
I KNOW ALL ABOUT YOUR SPINJITZU. DO YOU EXPECT ME TO BE AFRAID?
NO. I EXPECT YOU TO BE SMART.
BECAUSE THE NINDROIDS WON'T BE AS GENTLE AS ME.
WHUMP

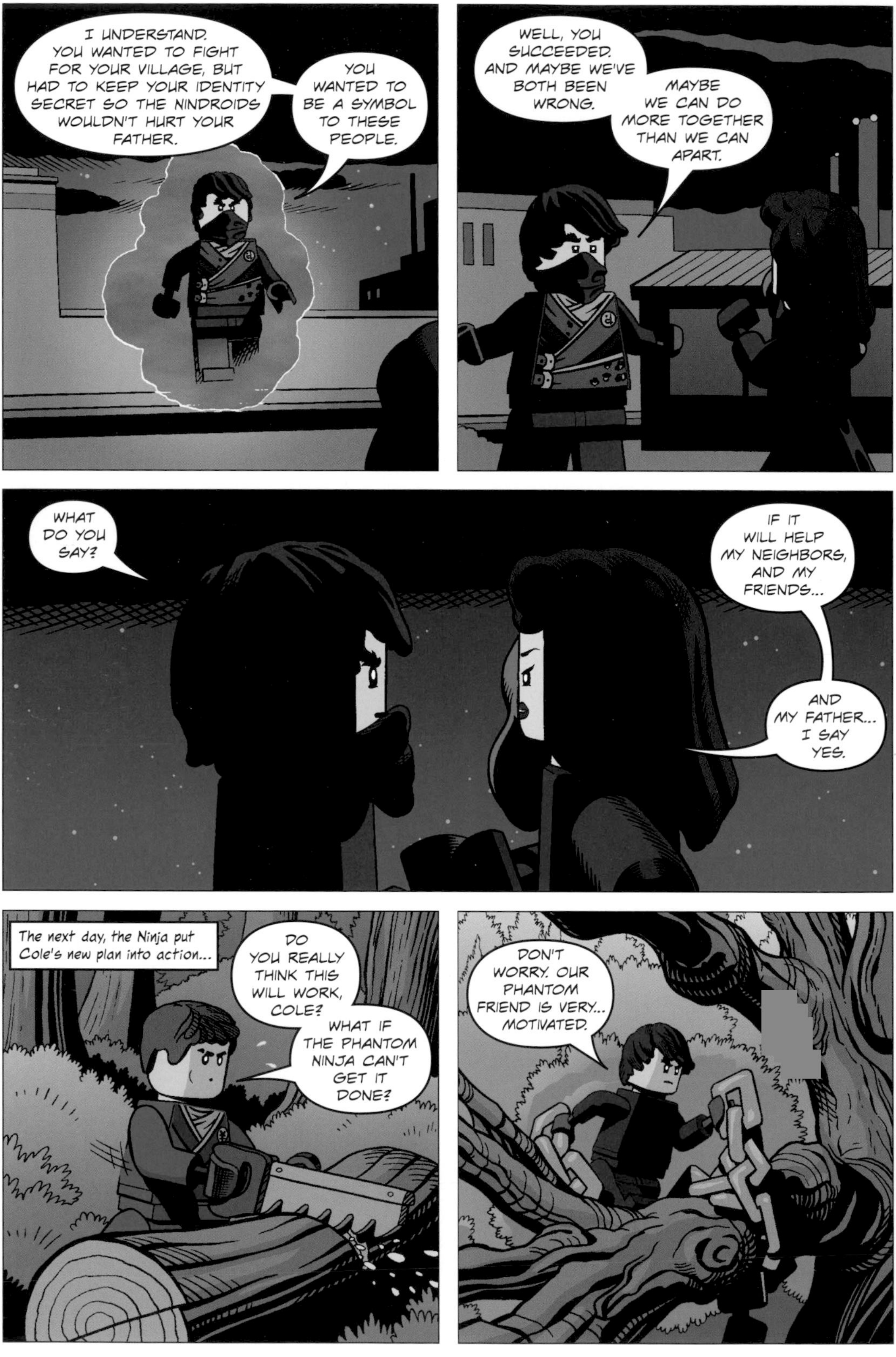
I UNDERSTAND. YOU WANTED TO FIGHT FOR YOUR VILLAGE, BUT HAD TO KEEP YOUR IDENTITY SECRET SO THE NINDROIDS WOULDN'T HURT YOUR FATHER.
YOU WANTED TO BE A SYMBOL TO THESE PEOPLE.
WELL, YOU SUCCEEDED. AND MAYBE WE'VE BOTH BEEN WRONG.
MAYBE WE CAN DO MORE TOGETHER THAN WE CAN APART.
WHAT DO YOU SAY?
IF IT WILL HELP MY NEIGHBORS, AND MY FRIENDS...
AND MY FATHER... I SAY YES.
The next day, the Ninja put Cole's new plan into action...
DO YOU REALLY THINK THIS WILL WORK, COLE?
WHAT IF THE PHANTOM NINJA CAN'T GET IT DONE?
DON'T WORRY. OUR PHANTOM FRIEND IS VERY... MOTIVATED.

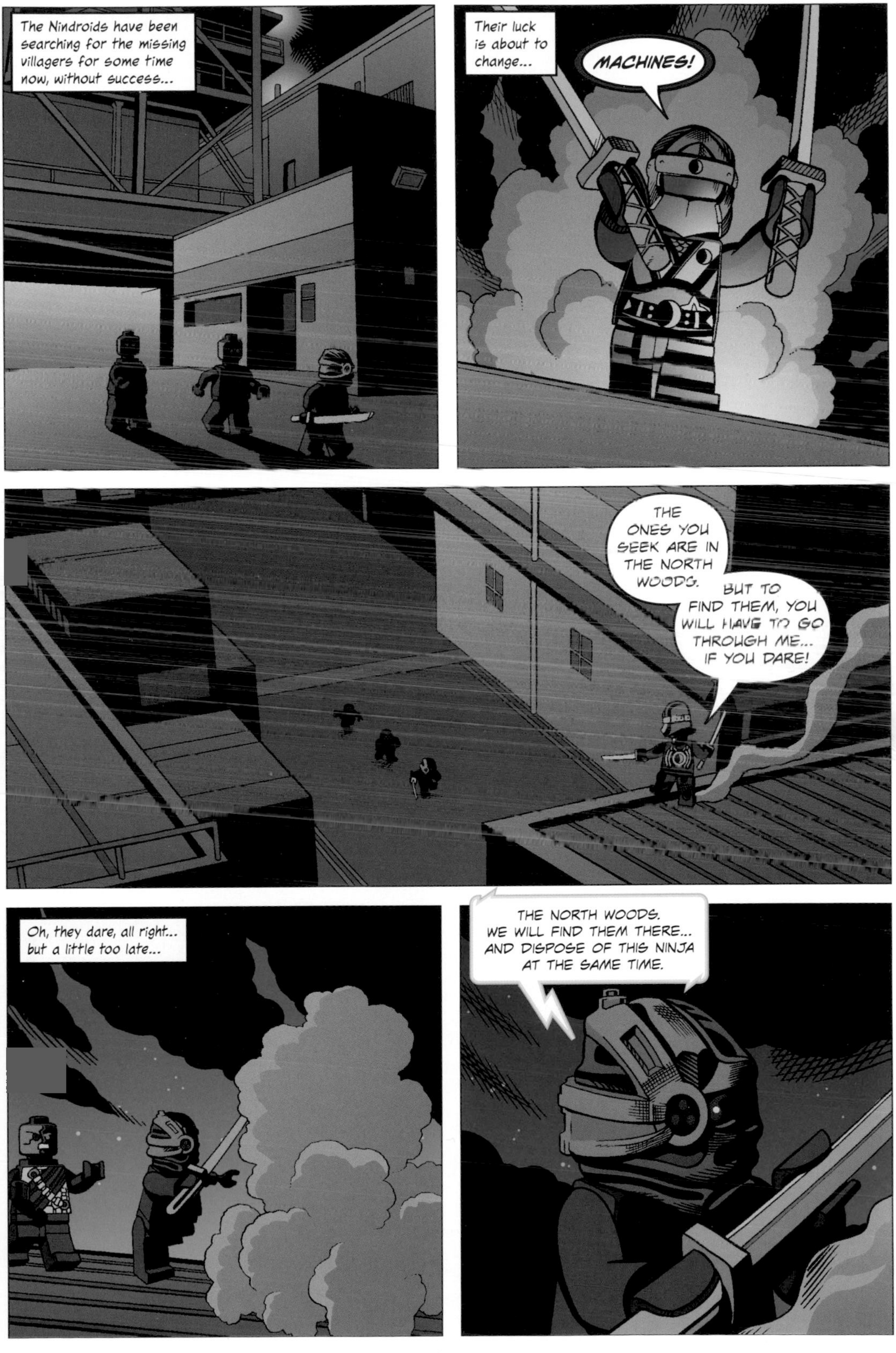
The Nindroids have been searching for the missing villagers for some time now, without success...
Their luck is about to change...
MACHINES!
THE ONES YOU SEEK ARE IN THE NORTH WOODS.
BUT TO FIND THEM, YOU WILL HAVE TO GO THROUGH ME... IF YOU DARE!
Oh, they dare, all right... but a little too late...
THE NORTH WOODS. WE WILL FIND THEM THERE... AND DISPOSE OF THIS NINJA AT THE SAME TIME.

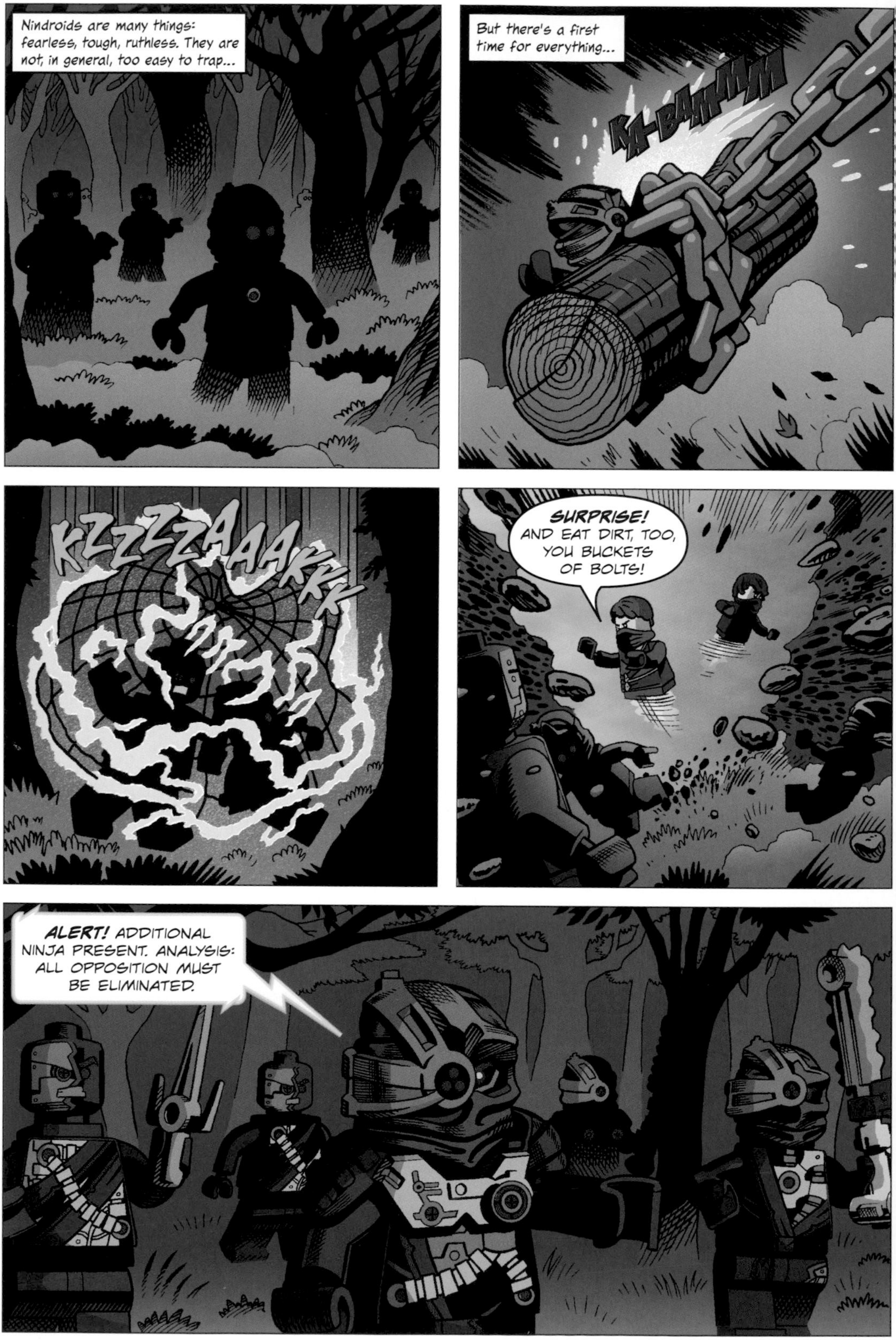
Nindroids are many things: fearless, tough, ruthless. They are not, in general, too easy to trap...
But there's a first time for everything...
KA-BAMMMM
KZZZZAAAKKK
SURPRISE! AND EAT DIRT, TOO, YOU BUCKETS OF BOLTS!
ALERT! ADDITIONAL NINJA PRESENT. ANALYSIS: ALL OPPOSITION MUST BE ELIMINATED.

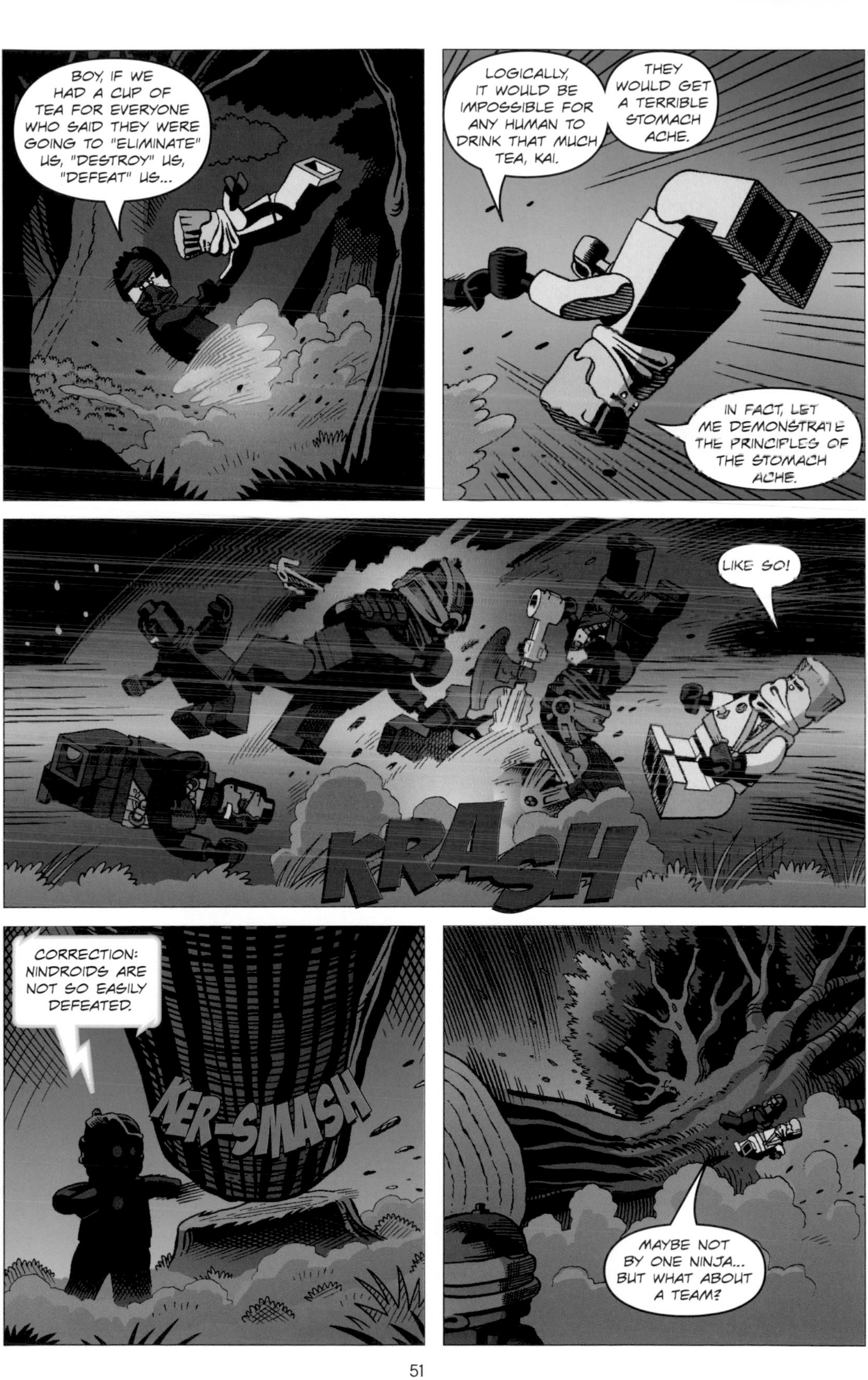
BOY, IF WE HAD A CUP OF TEA FOR EVERYONE WHO SAID THEY WERE GOING TO "ELIMINATE" US, "DESTROY" US, "DEFEAT" US...
LOGICALLY, IT WOULD BE IMPOSSIBLE FOR ANY HUMAN TO DRINK THAT MUCH TEA, KAI.
THEY WOULD GET A TERRIBLE STOMACH ACHE.
IN FACT, LET ME DEMONSTRATE THE PRINCIPLES OF THE STOMACH ACHE.
LIKE SO!
KRASH
CORRECTION: NINDROIDS ARE NOT SO EASILY DEFEATED.
KER-SMASH
MAYBE NOT BY ONE NINJA... BUT WHAT ABOUT A TEAM?

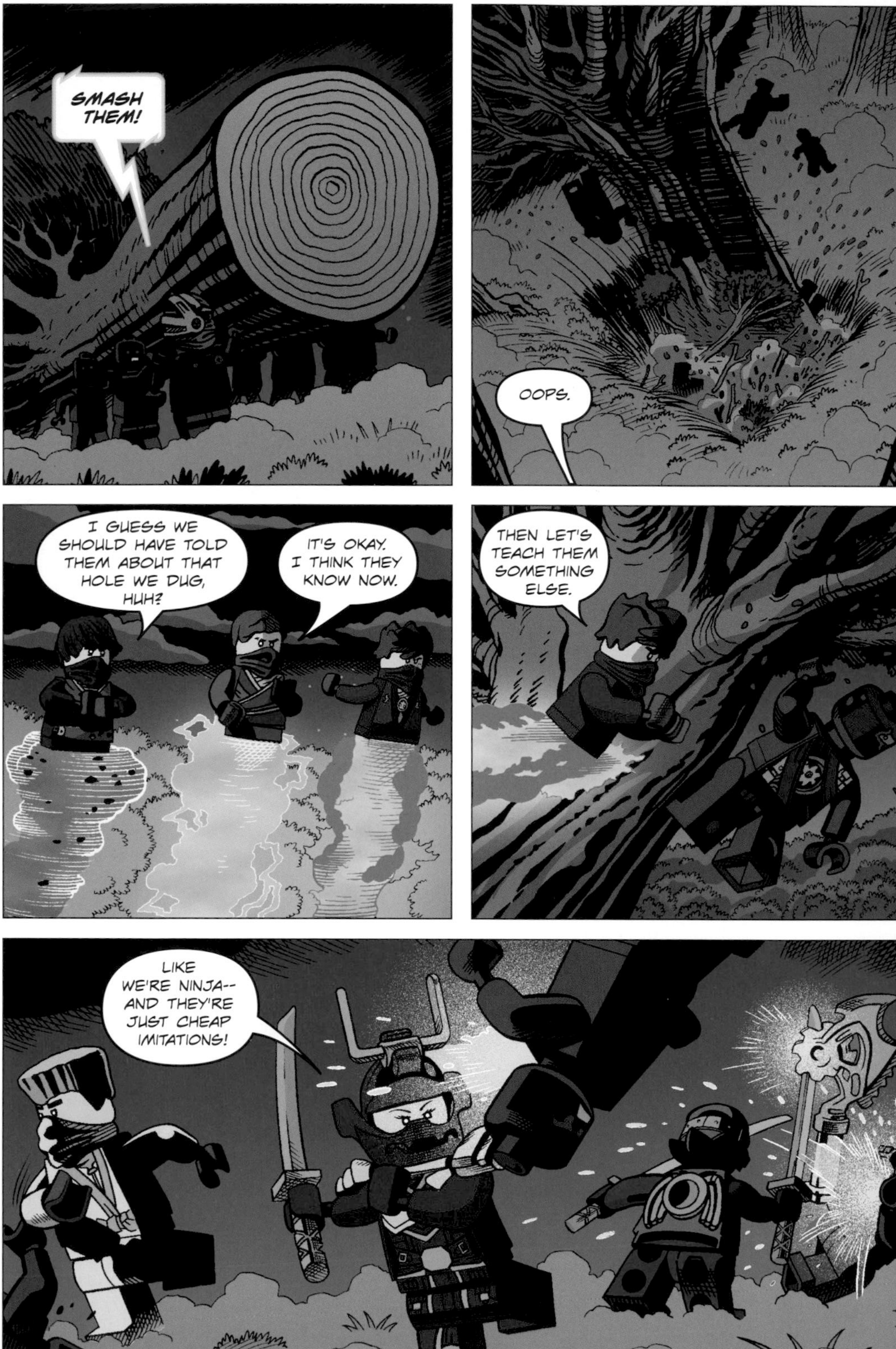
SMASH THEM!
OOPS.
I GUESS WE SHOULD HAVE TOLD THEM ABOUT THAT HOLE WE DUG, HUH?
IT'S OKAY. I THINK THEY KNOW NOW.
THEN LET'S TEACH THEM SOMETHING ELSE.
LIKE WE'RE NINJA-- AND THEY'RE JUST CHEAP IMITATIONS!

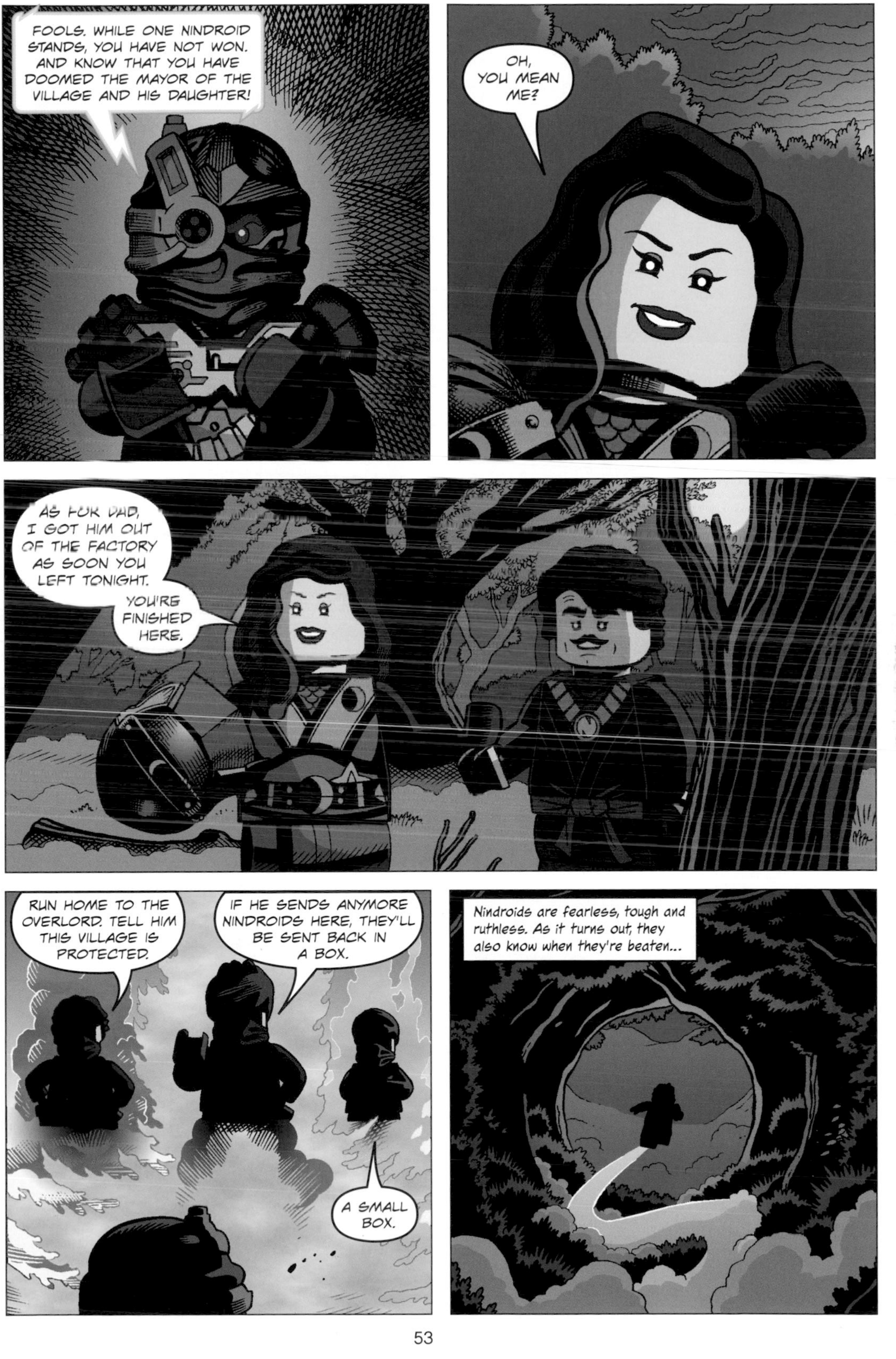
FOOLS. WHILE ONE NINDROID STANDS, YOU HAVE NOT WON. AND KNOW THAT YOU HAVE DOOMED THE MAYOR OF THE VILLAGE AND HIS DAUGHTER!
OH, YOU MEAN ME?
AS FOR DAD, I GOT HIM OUT OF THE FACTORY AS SOON YOU LEFT TONIGHT.
YOU'RE FINISHED HERE.
RUN HOME TO THE OVERLORD. TELL HIM THIS VILLAGE IS PROTECTED.
IF HE SENDS ANYMORE NINDROIDS HERE, THEY'LL BE SENT BACK IN A BOX.
A SMALL BOX.
Nindroids are fearless, tough and ruthless. As it turns out, they also know when they're beaten...

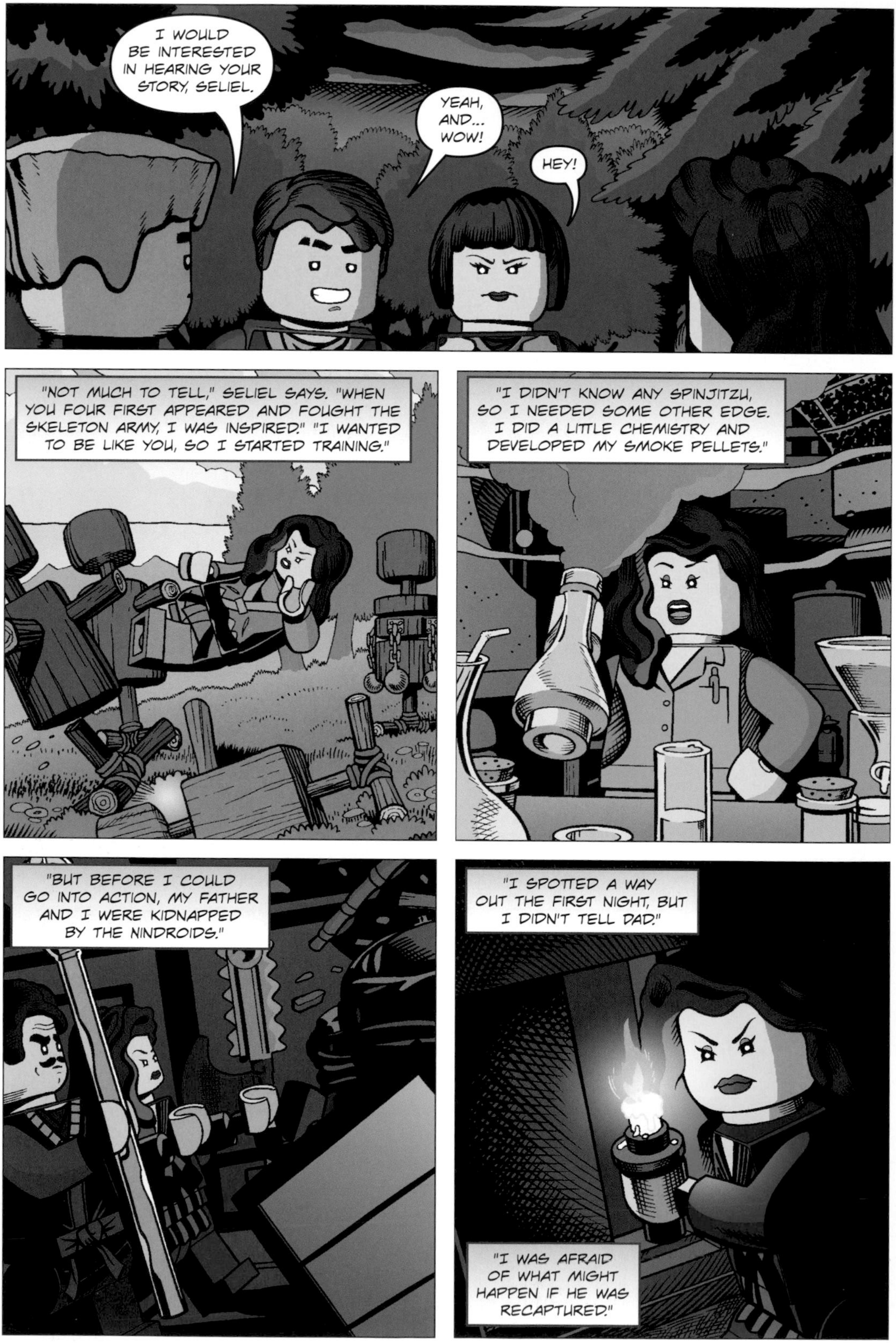
I WOULD BE INTERESTED IN HEARING YOUR STORY, SELIEL.
YEAH, AND... WOW!
HEY!
"NOT MUCH TO TELL," SELIEL SAYS. "WHEN YOU FOUR FIRST APPEARED AND FOUGHT THE SKELETON ARMY, I WAS INSPIRED." "I WANTED TO BE LIKE YOU, SO I STARTED TRAINING."
"I DIDN'T KNOW ANY SPINJITZU, SO I NEEDED SOME OTHER EDGE. I DID A LITTLE CHEMISTRY AND DEVELOPED MY SMOKE PELLETS."
"BUT BEFORE I COULD GO INTO ACTION, MY FATHER AND I WERE KIDNAPPED BY THE NINDROIDS."
"I SPOTTED A WAY OUT THE FIRST NIGHT, BUT I DIDN'T TELL DAD."
"I WAS AFRAID OF WHAT MIGHT HAPPEN IF HE WAS RECAPTURED."

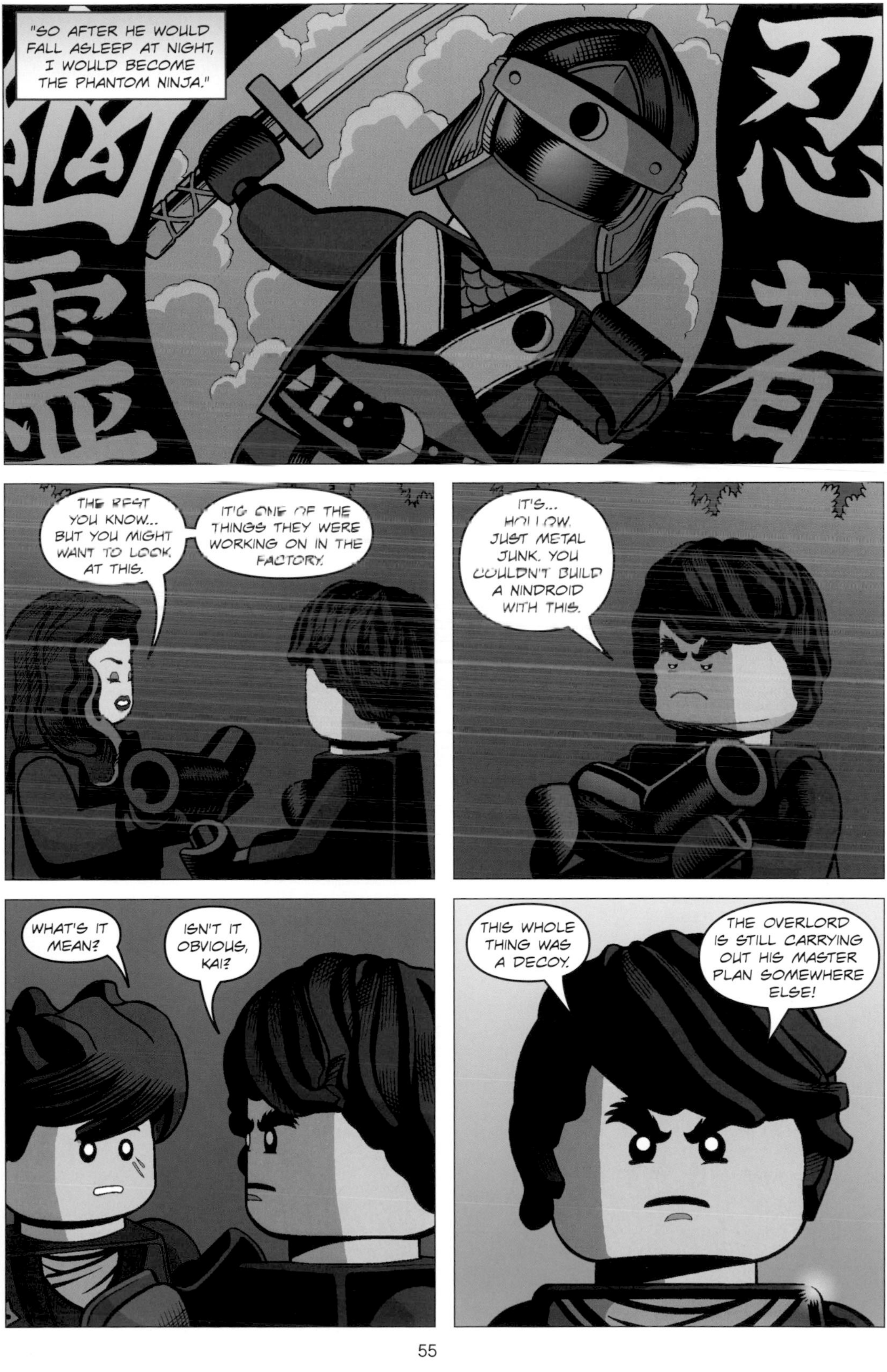
"SO AFTER HE WOULD FALL ASLEEP AT NIGHT, I WOULD BECOME THE PHANTOM NINJA."
忍者
幽霊
THE REST YOU KNOW... BUT YOU MIGHT WANT TO LOOK AT THIS.
IT'S ONE OF THE THINGS THEY WERE WORKING ON IN THE FACTORY.
IT'S... HOLLOW. JUST METAL JUNK. YOU COULDN'T BUILD A NINDROID WITH THIS.
WHAT'S IT MEAN?
ISN'T IT OBVIOUS, KAI?
THIS WHOLE THING WAS A DECOY.
THE OVERLORD IS STILL CARRYING OUT HIS MASTER PLAN SOMEWHERE ELSE!

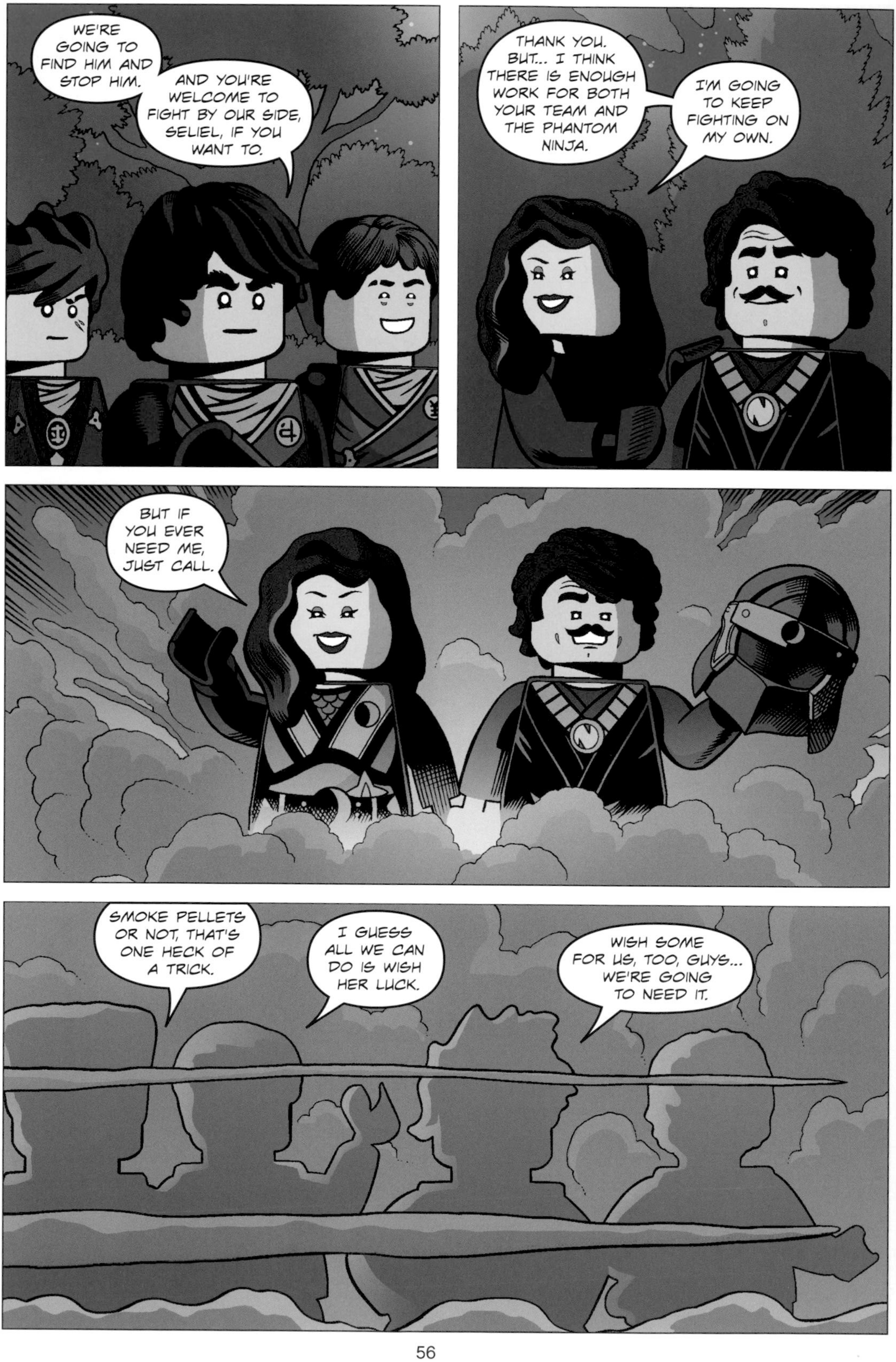
WE'RE GOING TO FIND HIM AND STOP HIM.
AND YOU'RE WELCOME TO FIGHT BY OUR SIDE, SELIEL, IF YOU WANT TO.
THANK YOU. BUT... I THINK THERE IS ENOUGH WORK FOR BOTH YOUR TEAM AND THE PHANTOM NINJA.
I'M GOING TO KEEP FIGHTING ON MY OWN.
BUT IF YOU EVER NEED ME, JUST CALL.
SMOKE PELLETS OR NOT, THAT'S ONE HECK OF A TRICK.
I GUESS ALL WE CAN DO IS WISH HER LUCK.
WISH SOME FOR US, TOO, GUYS... WE'RE GOING TO NEED IT.

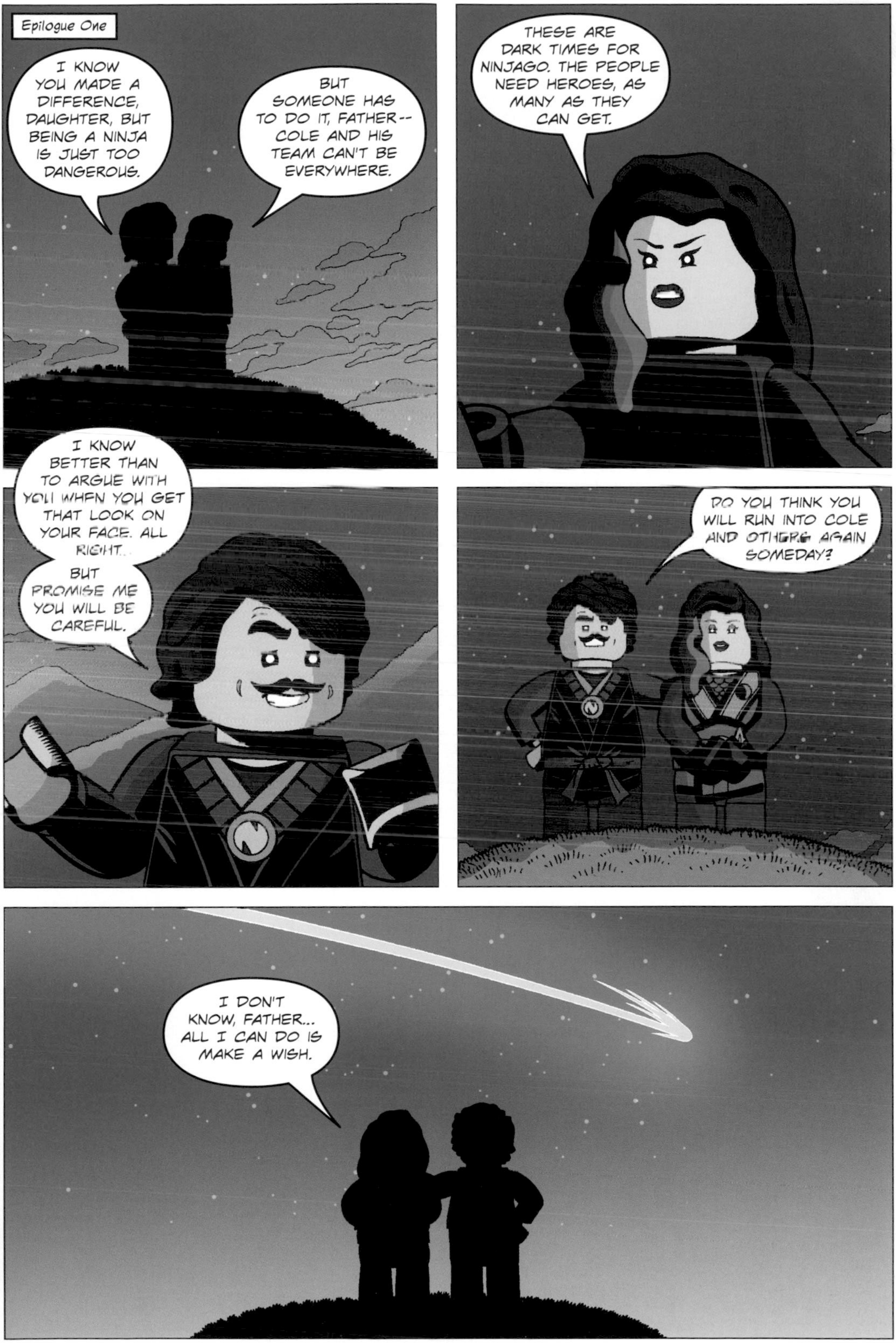
Epilogue One
I KNOW YOU MADE A DIFFERENCE, DAUGHTER, BUT BEING A NINJA IS JUST TOO DANGEROUS.
BUT SOMEONE HAS TO DO IT, FATHER-- COLE AND HIS TEAM CAN'T BE EVERYWHERE.
THESE ARE DARK TIMES FOR NINJAGO. THE PEOPLE NEED HEROES, AS MANY AS THEY CAN GET.
I KNOW BETTER THAN TO ARGUE WITH YOU WHEN YOU GET THAT LOOK ON YOUR FACE. ALL RIGHT...
BUT PROMISE ME YOU WILL BE CAREFUL.
DO YOU THINK YOU WILL RUN INTO COLE AND OTHERS AGAIN SOMEDAY?
I DON'T KNOW, FATHER... ALL I CAN DO IS MAKE A WISH.

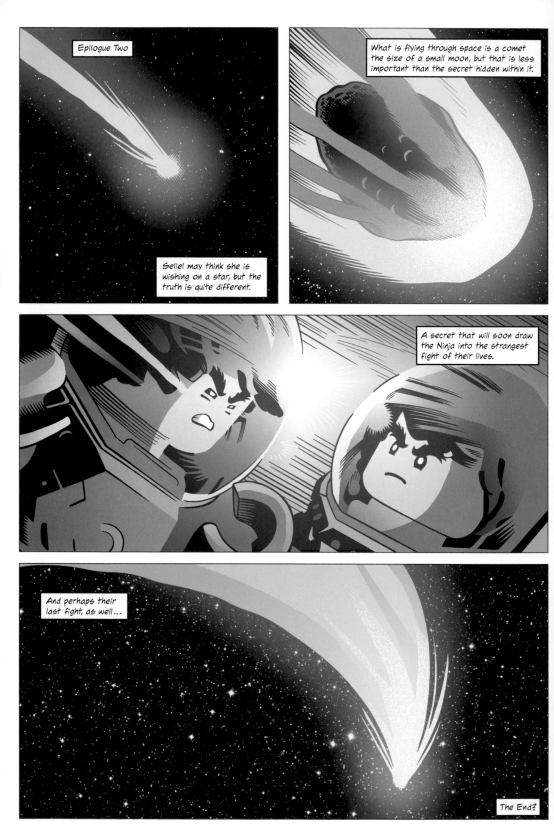

Epilogue Two

Seliel may think she is wishing on a star, but the truth is quite different.

What is flying through space is a comet the size of a small moon, but that is less important than the secret hidden within it.

A secret that will soon draw the Ninja into the strangest fight of their lives.

And perhaps their last fight, as well...

The End?

WATCH OUT FOR PAPERCUTZ™

Welcome to the everything-is-awesome, not to mention phantasmagorical, tenth LEGO ® NINJAGO graphic novel, by Greg Farshtey and Jolyon Yates, from Papercutz, the minitaure comics company dedicated to publishing great graphic novels for all ages. I'm Jim Salicrup, the enthusiastic Editor-in-Chief and first to order THE LEGO MOVIE on DVD!

There's so much super-eventful LEGO news to report, that I hardly know where to start! You probably already saw the amazing blockbuster hit THE LEGO MOVIE, and saw Lloyd's cameo as the Green Ninja. And if you were paying really close attention, you may've even glimpsed the BIONICLE ® appearance during the sequence when Wyldstyle mentions "sets we pretend never existed." (BIONICLE was the first LEGO graphic novel series from Papercutz, as you must already know, right?)

And of course, while THE LEGO MOVIE was #1 on all the box office charts, we're proud to say that LEGO NINJAGO #9 was #1 on The New York Times Graphic Books (paperbacks) best-sellers list! Congratulations to our creative crew of Greg Farshtey, awesome author, Jolyon Yates, awesome artist, Laurie E. Smith, awesome colorist, and Bryan Senka, awesome letterer!

And you know what else is awesome? How about the very first appearance of The Phantom Ninja anywhere? In the world of comicbooks, certain back issues are highly prized by collectors, such as ACTION COMICS #1, which featured the very first appearance of Superman, and DETECTIVE COMICS #27, which had the dramatic debut of Dark Knight Detective—Batman. ACTION COMICS #1, published in 1938 and priced at only ten cents per copy, now holds the record as the only single issue of a comicbook to have sold for over $2,000,000.00. DETECTIVE COMICS #27 has sold for over a million dollars and is catching up to ACTION #1. Now, we don't mean to imply that this LEGO NINJAGO graphic novel, featuring The Phantom Ninja is ever going to be worth over a million dollars, but you never know! Anything is possible. Suppose Ninjago fans fall in love with her and demand to see her return in the graphic novel series? (You can send your requests to me at the addresses below!) Imagine that she becomes so popular that fans then demand that she be featured on TV or in a movie with the Masters of Spinjitzu? Hey, The Green Ninja had his awesome cameo appearance in THE LEGO Movie, along with Superman and Batman! That could lead to her getting her own LEGO figure and who knows what else? But returning to reality for just a moment, The Phantom Ninja can just as easily be forgotten forever. It's ultimately all up to you.

Think I'm kidding? Then let me tell you about a fan named Micheal Uslan. He loved comics growing up, and one of the biggest turning points in his life was when Batman made the leap from comicbooks to TV back in 1966. Michael really had high hopes for the TV series, but was unhappy with the campy interpretation the producers went with for the prime-time series. Like Bruce Wayne, vowing revenge on all evil-doers to avenge the murder of his parents, Michael vowed he would one day get his vision of the grimmer, darker Batman to the big screen. And you know what? He did it! You can read all about it in his book, "The Boy Who Loved Batman." But to show that everything comes full circle—Micheal Uslan also is an Excutive Producer of THE LEGO MOVIE, which features a somewhat humorous, lighter, but still grim version of Batman.

But our biggest news for you is the announcement of another all-new LEGO graphic novel series from Papercutz! Because you demanded it, LEGO LEGENDS OF CHIMA™ is now an all-new graphic novel series from Papercutz! Just check out the preview on the following pages!

Whoops, I think I got a bit carried away talking about The Phantom Ninja! Now I don't have any room left to remark on the all-new second printing of LEGO NINJAGO #9 with all the ninja costumes redrawn. Or to mention that in the next LEGO NINJAGO graphic novels, the ninja are trapped in outer space in "Comet Crisis"—trust me, you don't want to miss it!

Jim

STAY IN TOUCH!
EMAIL: salicrup@papercutz.com
WEB: papercutz.com
TWITTER: @papercutzgn
FACEBOOK: PAPERCUTZGRAPHICNOVELS
FAN MAIL: Papercutz, 160 Broadway, Suite 700, East Wing,
                New York, NY 10038

Special Preview of LEGO LEGENDS OF CHIMA #1 "High Risk!"

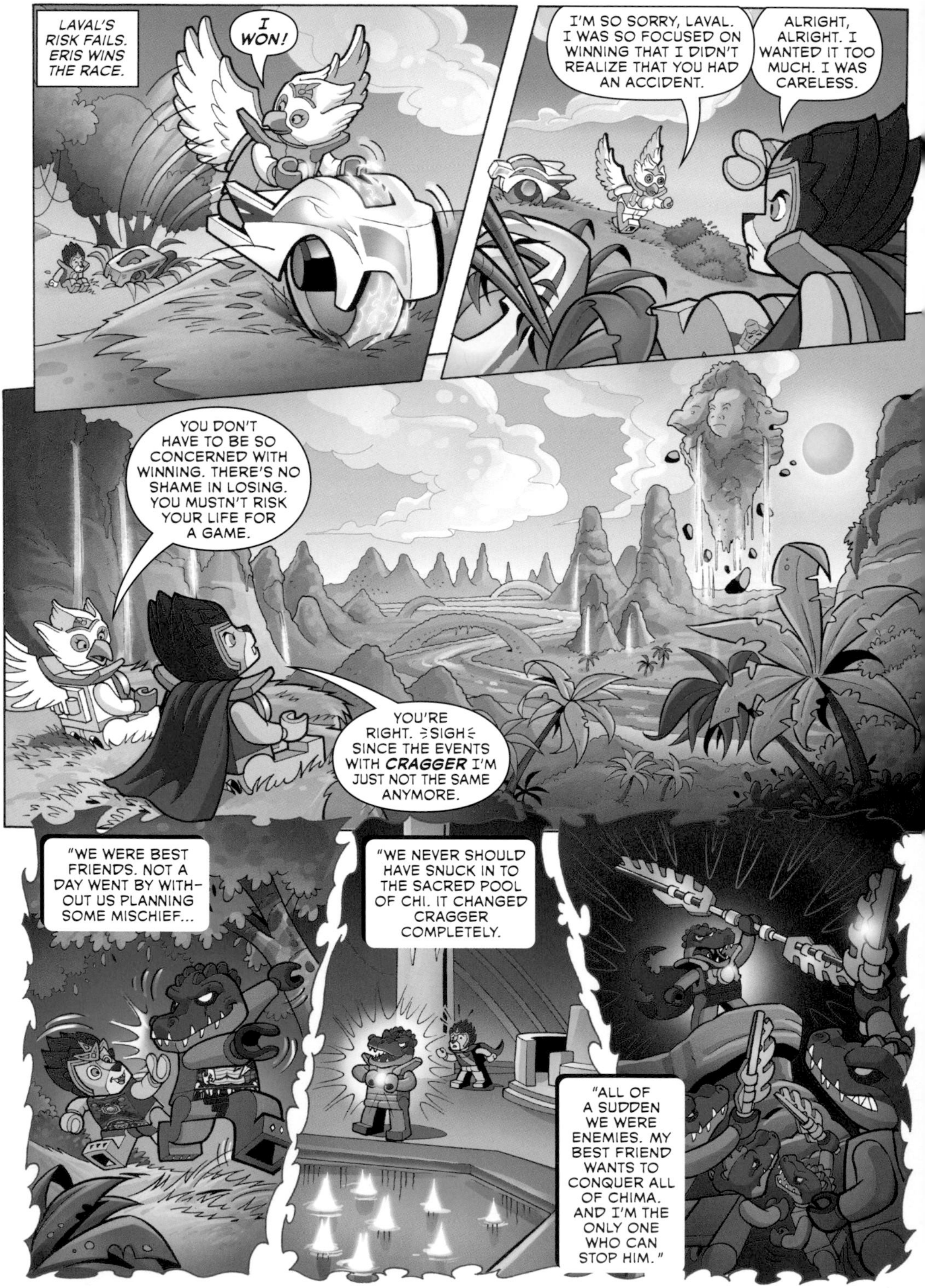
LAVAL'S RISK FAILS. ERIS WINS THE RACE.
I WON!
I'M SO SORRY, LAVAL. I WAS SO FOCUSED ON WINNING THAT I DIDN'T REALIZE THAT YOU HAD AN ACCIDENT.
ALRIGHT, ALRIGHT. I WANTED IT TOO MUCH. I WAS CARELESS.
YOU DON'T HAVE TO BE SO CONCERNED WITH WINNING. THERE'S NO SHAME IN LOSING. YOU MUSTN'T RISK YOUR LIFE FOR A GAME.
YOU'RE RIGHT. =SIGH= SINCE THE EVENTS WITH CRAGGER I'M JUST NOT THE SAME ANYMORE.
"WE WERE BEST FRIENDS. NOT A DAY WENT BY WITH-OUT US PLANNING SOME MISCHIEF...
"WE NEVER SHOULD HAVE SNUCK IN TO THE SACRED POOL OF CHI. IT CHANGED CRAGGER COMPLETELY.
"ALL OF A SUDDEN WE WERE ENEMIES. MY BEST FRIEND WANTS TO CONQUER ALL OF CHIMA. AND I'M THE ONLY ONE WHO CAN STOP HIM."

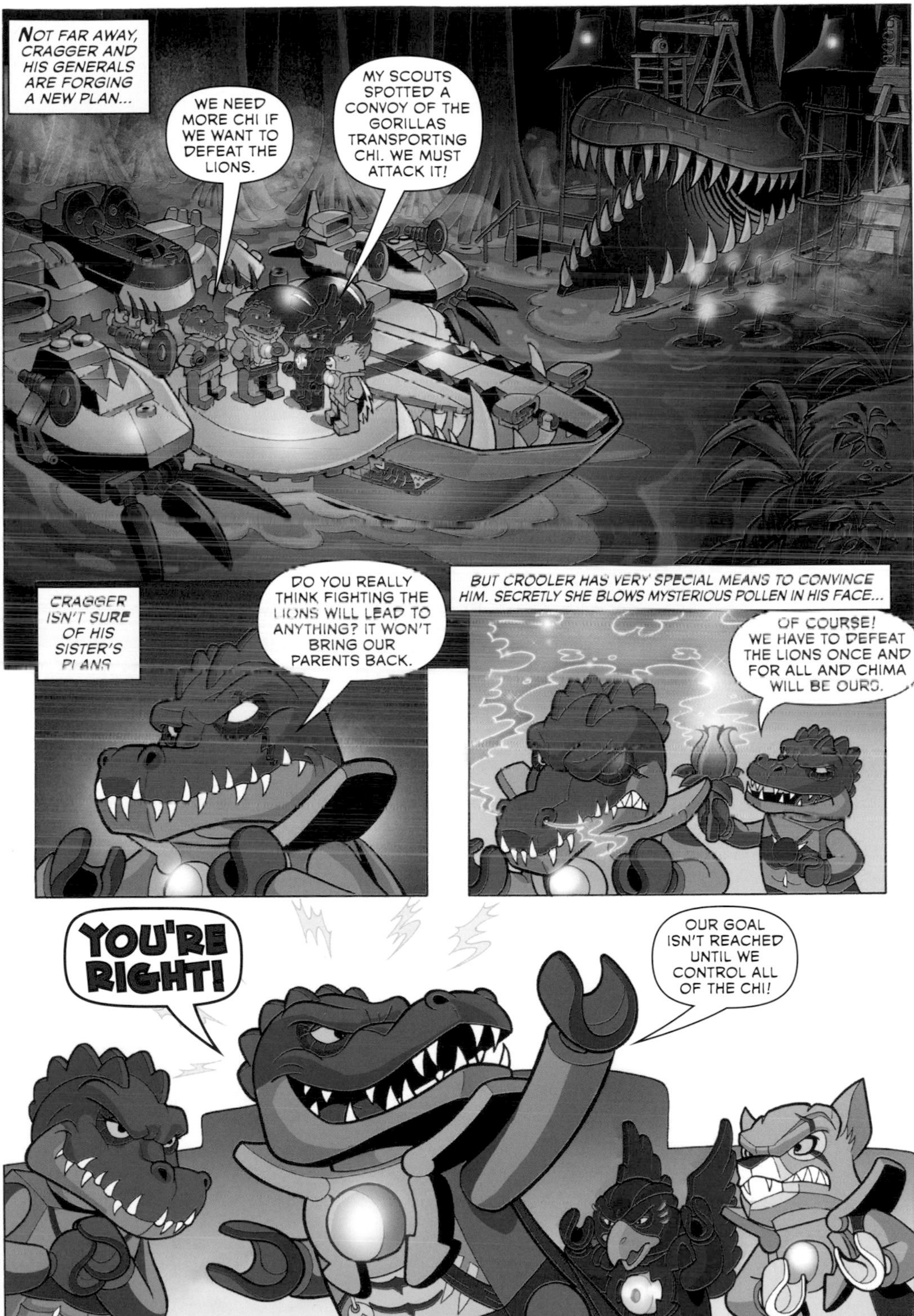
NOT FAR AWAY, CRAGGER AND HIS GENERALS ARE FORGING A NEW PLAN...
WE NEED MORE CHI IF WE WANT TO DEFEAT THE LIONS.
MY SCOUTS SPOTTED A CONVOY OF THE GORILLAS TRANSPORTING CHI. WE MUST ATTACK IT!
CRAGGER ISN'T SURE OF HIS SISTER'S PLANS
DO YOU REALLY THINK FIGHTING THE LIONS WILL LEAD TO ANYTHING? IT WON'T BRING OUR PARENTS BACK.
BUT CROOLER HAS VERY SPECIAL MEANS TO CONVINCE HIM. SECRETLY SHE BLOWS MYSTERIOUS POLLEN IN HIS FACE...
OF COURSE! WE HAVE TO DEFEAT THE LIONS ONCE AND FOR ALL AND CHIMA WILL BE OURS.
YOU'RE RIGHT!
OUR GOAL ISN'T REACHED UNTIL WE CONTROL ALL OF THE CHI!

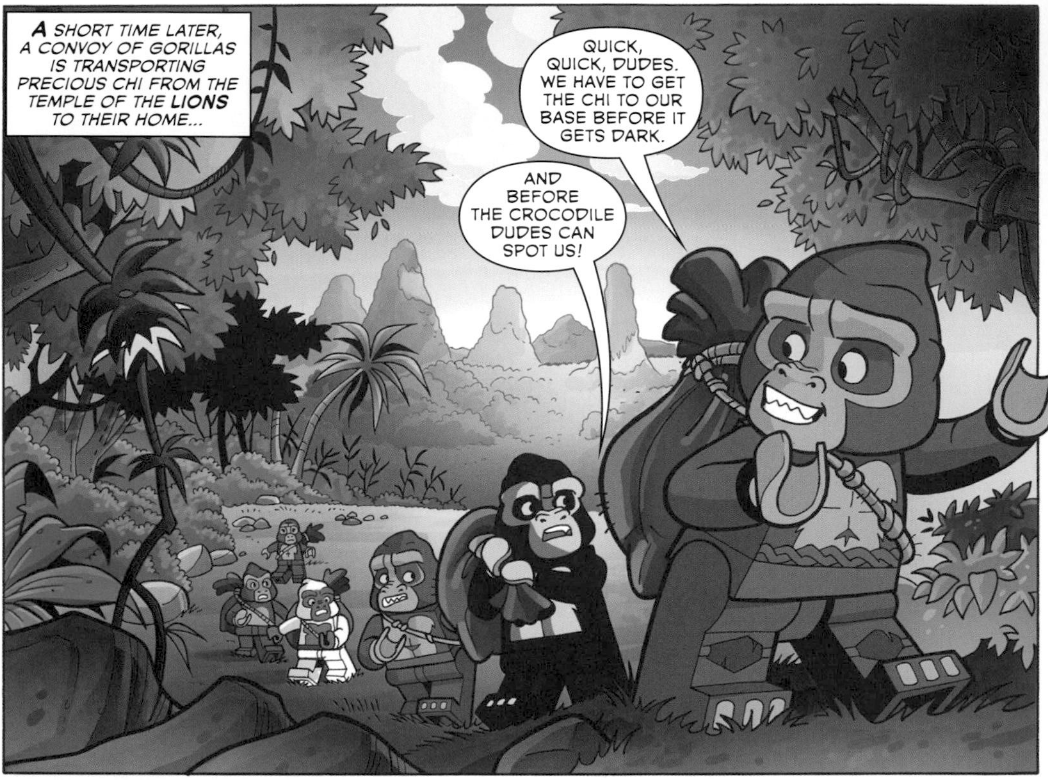
A SHORT TIME LATER, A CONVOY OF GORILLAS IS TRANSPORTING PRECIOUS CHI FROM THE TEMPLE OF THE LIONS TO THEIR HOME...
QUICK, QUICK, DUDES. WE HAVE TO GET THE CHI TO OUR BASE BEFORE IT GETS DARK.
AND BEFORE THE CROCODILE DUDES CAN SPOT US!

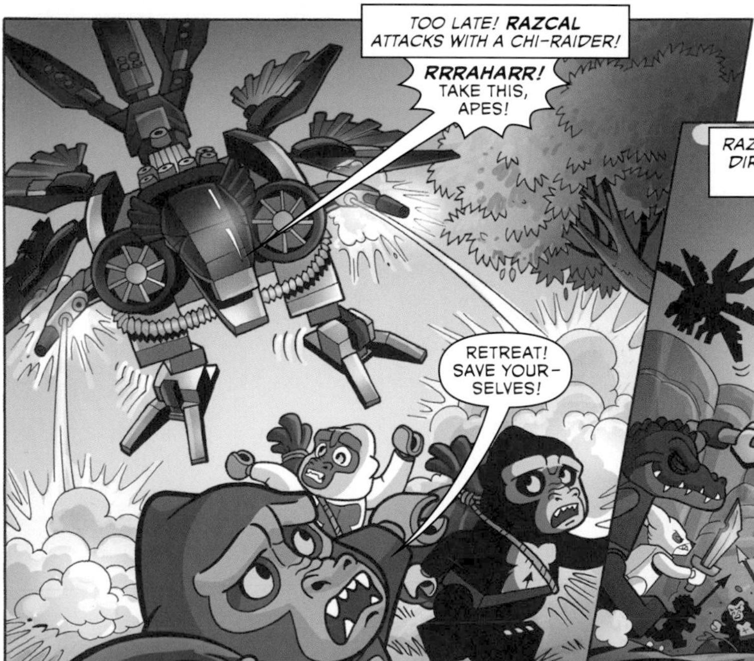
TOO LATE! RAZCAL ATTACKS WITH A CHI-RAIDER!
RRRAHARR! TAKE THIS, APES!
RETREAT! SAVE YOUR-SELVES!

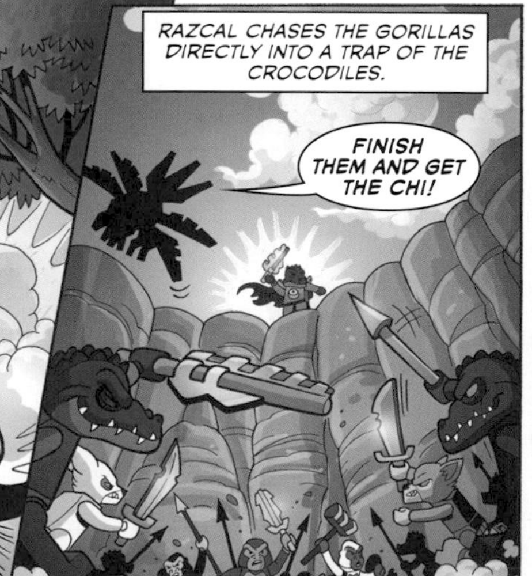
RAZCAL CHASES THE GORILLAS DIRECTLY INTO A TRAP OF THE CROCODILES.
FINISH THEM AND GET THE CHI!

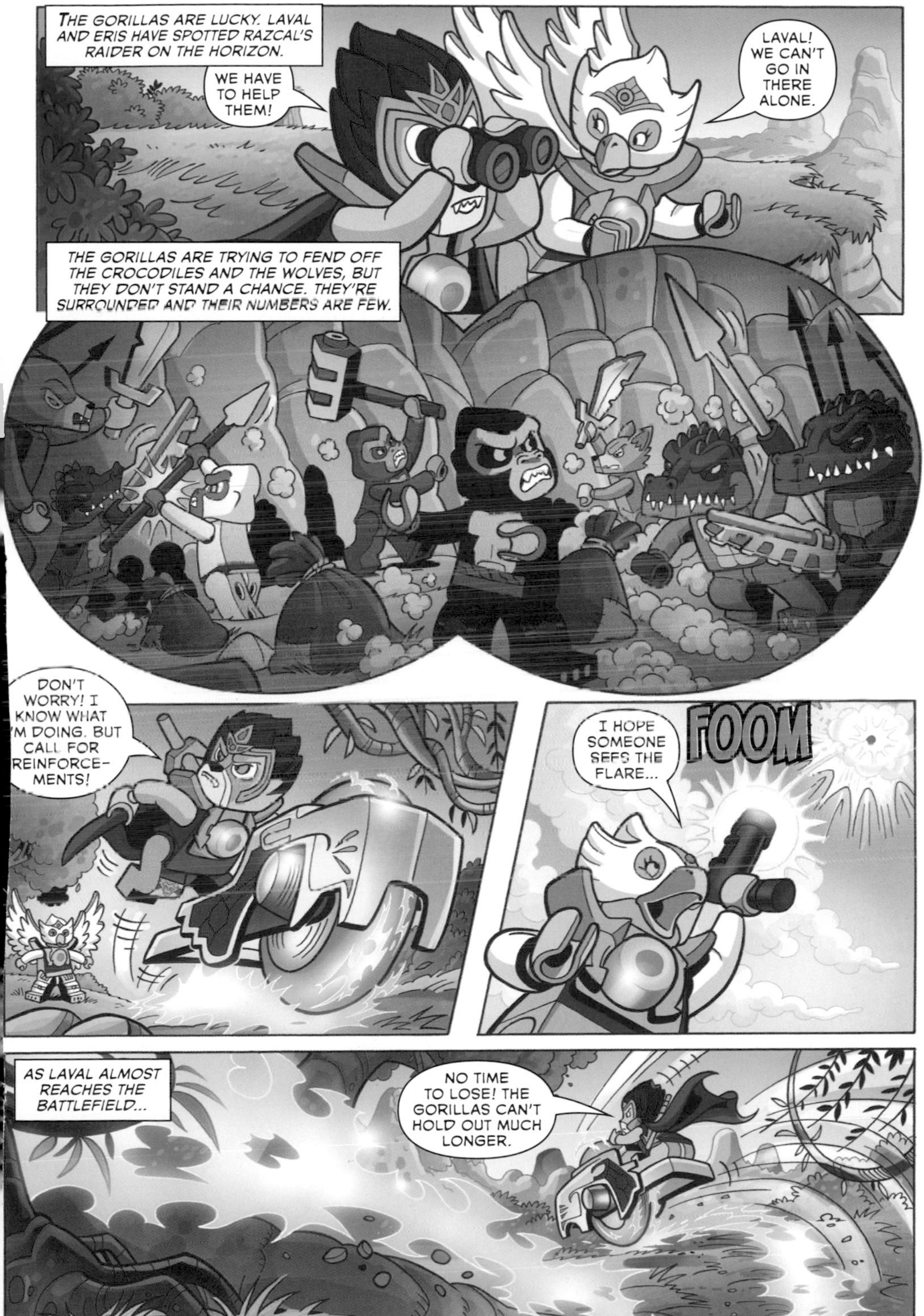

THE GORILLAS ARE LUCKY. LAVAL AND ERIS HAVE SPOTTED RAZCAL'S RAIDER ON THE HORIZON.
WE HAVE TO HELP THEM!
LAVAL! WE CAN'T GO IN THERE ALONE.
THE GORILLAS ARE TRYING TO FEND OFF THE CROCODILES AND THE WOLVES, BUT THEY DON'T STAND A CHANCE. THEY'RE SURROUNDED AND THEIR NUMBERS ARE FEW.
DON'T WORRY! I KNOW WHAT I'M DOING. BUT CALL FOR REINFORCEMENTS!
I HOPE SOMEONE SEES THE FLARE...
FOOM
AS LAVAL ALMOST REACHES THE BATTLEFIELD...
NO TIME TO LOSE! THE GORILLAS CAN'T HOLD OUT MUCH LONGER.

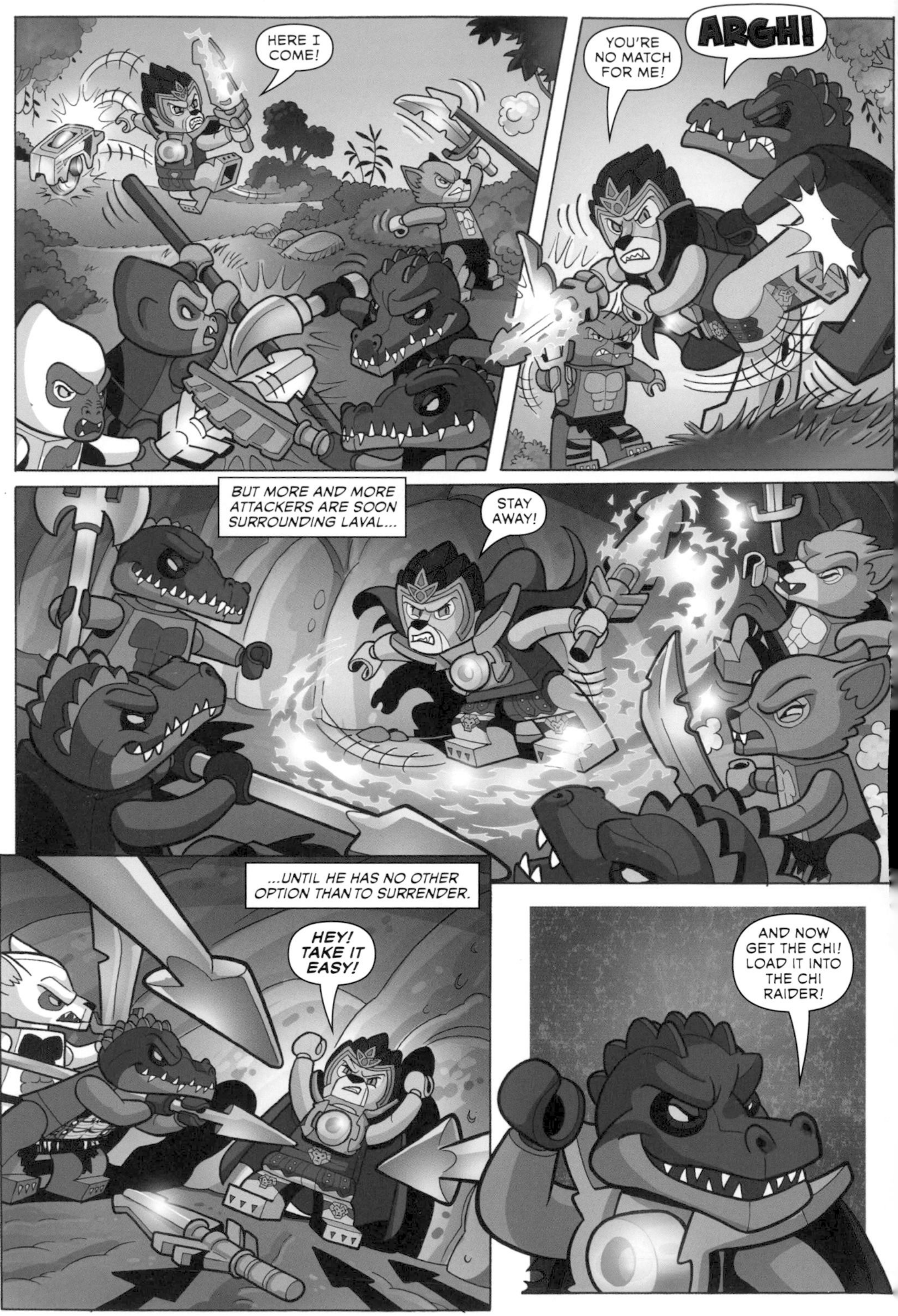
HERE I COME!
YOU'RE NO MATCH FOR ME!
ARGH!
BUT MORE AND MORE ATTACKERS ARE SOON SURROUNDING LAVAL...
STAY AWAY!
...UNTIL HE HAS NO OTHER OPTION THAN TO SURRENDER.
HEY! TAKE IT EASY!
AND NOW GET THE CHI! LOAD IT INTO THE CHI RAIDER!

For The Thrill-Packed Conclusion,
Don't Miss LEGO LEGENDS OF CHIMA #1 "High Risk!"

LEGO® NINJAGO Masters of Spinjitzu
#10 "The Phantom Ninja"
Greg Farshtey – Writer
Jolyon Yates – Artist
Laurie E. Smith – Colorist
Bryan Senka – Letterer
"High Risk" Preview
Yannick Grotholt – Writer
Comicon
(Miguel Sánchez – Pencils
Marc Alberich – Inker
Oriol San Julian – Colorist) – Artists
Tom Orzechowski – Letterer
Dawn K. Guzzo – Production
Beth Scorzato – Production Coordinator
Michael Petranek – Associate Editor
Jim Salicrup
Editor-in-Chief

ISBN: 978-1-59707-718-7 paperback edition
ISBN: 978-1-59707-719-4 hardcover edition

Papercutz books may be purchased for business or promotional use. For information on bulk purchases please contact Macmillan Corporate and Premium Sales Department at (800) 221-7945 x5442.

Printed in Canada
May 2014 by Friesens Printing
1 Printers Way
Altona, MB R0G 0B0

Distributed by Macmillan
First Printing

THE PHANTOM NINJA

Greg Farshtey – Writer

Jolyon Yates – Artist

Laurie E. Smith – Colorist

New York